THE FIVE GOLD BANDS

THE FIVE GOLD BANDS

Jack Vance

UNDERWOOD-MILLER
Novato, California
Lancaster, Pennsylvania
1993

THE FIVE GOLD BANDS
Trade edition ISBN 0-88733-159-9
Signed edition ISBN 0-88733-160-2

Jacket type and design by Arnie Fenner
Book design: Underwood-Miller
Printed in the United States of America
All Rights Reserved

Library of Congress Cataloging-in-Publication Data
Vance, Jack, 1916—
The five gold bands / Jack Vance.
      p. cm.
    ISBN 0-88733-159-9 : $24.95
    I. Title.
PS3572.A42F58   1993
813' .54—dc20
                                              93-14671
                                                    CIP

(SciFic)

THE FIVE GOLD BANDS

I

The tunnel ran through layers of red and gray sandstone cemented with silica-tough digging even with the patent grab-compactor. Twice Paddy Blackthorn had broken into old wells, once into a forgotten graveyard. Archaeologists would have chewed their fingernails to see Paddy crunching aside the ancient bones with his machine. Three hundred years of tunnel and the last six feet were the worst—two yards of feather delicate explosive, layers of steel, copper, durible, concrete, films of guard circuits.

Edging between the pockets of explosive, melting out the steels, leaching the concrete with acid, tenderly shorting across the alarm circuits, Paddy finally pierced the last layer of durable and pushed up the composition flooring.

He hauled himself up into the most secret spot of the known universe, played his flash around the room.

Drab concrete walls, dark floor—then the light glinted on ranks of metal tubes. "Doesn't that make a pretty sight, now," Paddy murmured raptly.

7

He moved—the light picked out a cubical frame supporting complexities of glass and wire, placket and durible, metal and manicloid.

"There it *is!*" said Paddy, his eyes lambent with triumph. "Now if only I could pull it back out the tunnel, then wouldn't I lord it over the high and mighty!...But no, that's a sweet dream; I'll content myself with mere riches. First to see if it'll curl out the blue flame...."

He stepped gingerly around the mechanism, peering into the interior. "Where's the button that says 'Push'...There's no clue—ah, *here!*" And Paddy advanced on the control panel. It was divided into five segments, each of which bore three dials calibrated from 0 to 1,000 and, below, the corresponding control knobs. Paddy inspected the panel for a moment, then turned back to the machine.

"There's the socket," he muttered, "and here's one of the pretty bright tubes to fit.... Now I throw the switches—and if she's set on the right readings, then I'm the most fortunate man ever out of Skibbereen, County Cork. So—I'll try her out." On each of the five panels he flung home the switches and stood back, playing his light expectantly on the metal tube.

Nothing happened. There was no quiver of energy, no flicker of sky-blue light whirling into a core down the center of the tube.

"Sacred heart!" muttered Paddy. "Is it that I've tunneled all this time for the joy of it? Och, there's one of three things the matter. The power's disconnected, or there's a master switch yet to be thrown. Or third and worst the dials are at their wrong settings." He rubbed at his chin. "Never say die, it's the power. There's none coming into the entire gargus." He turned his light around the room. "Now there's the power leads and they run into that little antechamber."

He peered through the arch. "Here's the master switch and just as I told all who had ears to listen it's open. Now—I'll close it and then we'll see.... Whisht a while. First, am I safe? I'll stand behind this bar-block and push home with this bit of pipe. Then I'll go in and play those dials like Biddy on the bobbins."

He pushed. In the other room fifteen tongues of purple flame curled frantically out of the metal tube, lashed at the walls, fused the machinery, flung masonry at the bar-block, made chaos in a circle a hundred feet wide.

When the Kudthu guards probed the wreckage Paddy was struggling feebly behind the dented bar-block, a tangle of copper tubing across the legs.

Akhabats' jail was a citadel of old brown brick, hugging the top of Jailhouse Hill like a scab on a sore thumb. Dust and the dull texture of the bricks gave the illusion of ruins, baking to rubble in the heat of Properus. Actually, the walls stood thick, cool, firm. Below to the south lay the dingy town. To the north were the Akhabats space yards. Beyond stretched the plain, flat and blue as mildew—as far as the eye could reach.

The Kudthu jailer woke Paddy by running horny fingers along the bars. "Earther, wake up."

Paddy arose, feeling his throat. "No need to break a man's sleep for a hanging. I'd be here in the morning."

"Come, no talk," rumbled the jailer, a manlike creature eight feet tall with rough gray skin, eyes like blue satin pin cushions where a true man's cheeks would have been.

Paddy stepped out into the aisle, followed the jailer past rows of other cells, whence came snores, rumblings, the luminous stare of eye, the hiss of scale on stone.

He was taken to a low brick-walled room, cut in half by a counter of dark bronze wax-wood. Beyond, around a long low table, sat a dozen figures more or less manlike. A mutter of conversation died as Paddy was brought forward and a row of eyes swung to stare at him.

"Ah, ye sculpins," muttered Paddy. "So you've come all the way to jeer at a poor Earther and his only sin was stealing space-drives. Well, stare then and be damned!" He squared his shoulders, glanced down the long table from face to face.

The Kudthu jailer pushed Paddy a little forward, and said, "This is the talker Lord Councillors."

The hooded Shaul Councillor, after a moment's scrutiny, said in the swift Shaul dialect, "What is your crime?"

"There's no crime, my Lord," replied Paddy in the same tongue. "I am innocent. I was but seeking my ship in the darkness and I fell into an old well and then—"

The jailor said, fumbling the words, "He was trying to steal space-drives, Lord Councillor."

"Mandatory death." The Shaul raked Paddy with eyes like tiny lights. "When is the execution?"

"Tomorrow, Lord, by hanging."

"The trial was over-hasty, Lord," exclaimed Paddy. "The famous Langtry justice has been scamped."

The councillor shrugged. "Can you speak each of the tongues of the Line?"

"They're like my own breath, Lord! I know them like I know the face of my old mother!"

The Shaul Councillor sat back in his seat. "You speak Shaul well enough."

The Koton Councillor spoke in the throaty Koton speech. "Do you understand me?"

Paddy replied, "Indeed I believe I am the only Earther alive that appreciates the beauty of your lovely tongue."

The Alpheratz Eagle asked the same question in his own lip-clacking talk. Paddy responded fluently.

The Badau and the Loristanese each spoke and Paddy replied to each.

There was a moment of silence during which Paddy looked right and left, hoping to seize a gun from a guard and kill all in the room. The guards wore no guns.

The Shaul asked, "How is it you are master of so many tongues?"

Paddy said, "My Lord, it's a habit with me. I've been journeying space since I was a lad and no sooner am I hearing strange speech than I'm wondering what's going on. And may I ask why it is you're questioning me? Are you grooming me for a pardon perhaps?"

"By no means," replied the Shaul. "Your offense is beyond pardon, it cuts at the base of the Langtry power. The punishment must be severe, to deter future offenders."

"Ah, but your Lordships," Paddy remonstrated, "it's you Langtrys who are the offenders. If you allowed your poor cousins on Earth more than our miserable ten drives, then a stolen drive would not bring a million marks and there'd be no temptation for us poor unfortunates."

"I do not see the quotas, Earther. That is in the hands of the Sons. Besides there are always scoundrels to steal ships and unmounted drives." He fixed Paddy with a significant glance.

The Koton Councillor said abruptly, "The man is mad."

"Mad?" The Shaul studied Paddy. "I doubt it. He is voluble—irreverent—unprincipled. But he appears sane."

"Unlikely." The Koton swung his thin gray-white arm across the table and handed the Shaul a sheet of paper. "This is his psychograph."

The Shaul studied it and the skin of his cowl rippled slowly.

"It is indeed odd...unprecedented...even allowing for the normal confusion of the Earth mind..." He glanced at Paddy. "Are you made?"

Paddy shrugged. "I take it I'd hang in any event."

The Shaul smiled grimly. "He is sane." He looked around at his fellows. "If there is no further objection then..." None of the Councillors spoke. The Shaul turned to the jailer.

"Handcuff him well, blindfold him—have him out on the platform in twenty minutes."

"Where's the priest?" yelled Paddy. "Get me the Holy Father from Saint Alban's. Are you for hauling me up without the sacrament?"

The Shaul gestured. "Take him."

Muttering wild curses Paddy was handcuffed, blindfolded, crow-legged out into the sharp night air. The wind, smelling of lichen, dry oil-grass, smoke, cut at his face. They led him up a ramp into a warm interior that felt solid, metallic. Paddy knew by the smell, compounded of oil, ozone, acryl varnish, and by the vague throb and vibration of much machinery, that he was aboard a large ship of space.

They led him to the cargo hold, removed the handcuffs, the blindfold. He looked wildly toward the door but the way was blocked by a pair of Kudthu attendants, watching him with blue-bottle eyes. So Paddy relaxed, stretched his sore muscles. The Kudthu attendants departed, the port swung shut, the dogs scraped down tight on the outside.

Paddy inspected his quarters—a metal-walled room about twenty feet in each direction, empty except for his own person.

"Well," said Paddy, "there's nothing to it. Complaints and protests will do me no good. If them Kudthu devils had been a quarter-ton lighter apiece, there might have been a fight."

He lay on the floor and presently the ship trembled, took to the air. The steady drone of the generator permeated the metal and Paddy went to sleep.

He was roused by a Shaul in the pink and blue garb of the Scribe caste. The Shaul was about his own size with a head shrouded by a cowl of fish-colored skin. It was attached at his shoulders, his neck, the back of his scalp and projected over his forehead in a widow's-peak of flexible black flesh. He carried a tray which he set on the floor beside Paddy.

"Your breakfast, Earther. Fried meat with salt, a salad of bog-greens."

"What kind of meat?" demanded Paddy. "Where did it come from? Akhabats?"

"Stores came aboard at Akhabats," admitted the Shaul.

"Away with it, you hooded scoundrel! There's never a bite of meat on the planet except that of the Kudthus that's died of old age. Be off with your cannibal food!"

The Shaul flapped his cowl without rancor. "Here's some fruit and some yeast cake and a pot of hot brew."

Grumbling, Paddy ate his breakfast, drank the hot liquid. And the Shaul watched him with a smile.

Paddy looked up, frowned. "And why then your crafty grin?"

"I merely observe that you appear to enjoy that broth."

Paddy set down the cup, coughed and spat. "Ah, you devil. Once that your tribe broke loose from Earth they forgot all decency and manners. Would I be feeding you with ghoul-food? Would I now, was we reversed?"

"Meat is meat," observed the Shaul, gathering the utensil. "You Earthers are oddly emotional about trivialities."

"By no means," declared Paddy. "We're the civilized ones of the universe in spite of your pretensions. It's you far-off heathens that have brought Mother Earth to her knees."

"Old stock must give way to newer types," said the Shaul mildly. "First the Pithecanthropi, then the Neanderthals, now the Earthers."

"Pah!" Paddy spat. "Give me thirty feet of flat ground with a bit of spring to it and I'll whip any five of you skinheads and any two of them Kudthu hunks."

The Shaul smiled faintly. "You Earthers don't even thieve well. After two months tunneling you're not five minutes in the building before you blow it up. Lucky there was only a trickle of current coming in or you'd have flattened the city."

"Sorry," sneered Paddy. "We Earthers only invented space-drive in the first place."

"Langtry discovered space-drive—and that by accident."

"And where'd you be without him?" asked Paddy. "You freak races are coasting on what Old Earth gave out to you in the first place."

Said the Shaul, smiling, "Answer me this—what may be the fifth root of a hundred and twelve?"

"Let me ask you," said Paddy craftily, "because you worked the sum just now before you came in. Now give me the seventh root of five thousand."

The Shaul closed his eyes, brought into his visual imagination a mental picture of a slide-rule, manipulated it mentally, read the answer. "Somewhere between three point three seven and three point three eight."

"Prove it," Paddy challenged.

"I'll give you a pencil and paper and you may prove it," said the Shaul.

Paddy compressed his lips. "Since you're so knowledgeable perhaps you'll know where we're off to and what it is they're wanting with me?"

"Certainly," said the Shaul. "The Sons of Langtry are holding their yearly council and you are to interpret for them."

"Sacred heart!" gasped Paddy. "How is this again?"

The Shaul said patiently, "Every year the Sons from the Five Worlds meet to arrange quotas and distribution of space-drives. Since regrettably there is jealousy and suspicion between the Five Worlds no single tongue is spoken. The Sons of the other four worlds would lose face.

"An interpreter is an easy expedient. He translates every word into four other tongues. The Sons gain time to reflect, there is complete impartiality and no damage to planetary pride."

The Shaul laughed silently a moment, then continued. "The interpreter, you must understand, performs no critical service since each of the Sons knows—to some extent—the tongue of the other four. He is merely a symbol of equality and even-based cooperation, a lubricant between the easily offended Sons."

Paddy rubbed his chin doubtfully. He said in a hushed voice, "But this proceeding is the secret of the galaxy. No one knows when or where it occurs. It's like the rendezvous of shameful lovers for the secrecy."

"Correct," said the Shaul. He eyed Paddy with bright meaningful eyes. "As you may be aware, many of the archaic races are dissatisfied with the quotas; the Sons of Langtry gathered together make a tempting target for assassination."

Paddy gestured expressively. "Why am I selected for the honor? Surely there are others fully equal to it?"

"Yes indeed," agreed the Shaul. "I, for instance, speak each of the five tongues fluently. However I am no criminal condemned to death."

Paddy nodded with deep comprehension. "I see, I see. And suppose I refuse to serve as the mouthpiece, then what?"

"They put you through the nerve-suit once or twice, and generally you are eager for any chance at a quick death."

"Ah, the ugly creatures," groaned Paddy. "A man's will is no longer his own in these sad times."

The Shaul rose to his feet, picked up the dishes with fingers long and slender as pencils. He left the hold and a few moments later returned.

"Now, Earther, I must instruct you in the proper ceremonial. Certain of the Sons are insistent on decorum. Luckily—since we arrive at the rendezvous tomorrow—there is little to learn."

II

The Shaul awoke Paddy the next day with his breakfast, a razor, a mist-bulb, fresh linen, a pair of thick-soled sandals. Paddy hefted the last questioningly.

"You'll be walking on rock," the Shaul explained.

Paddy shaved, stripped, cleansed himself with the spray from the mist-bulb, stepped into fresh garments. He stretched his arms, felt his face.

"Now, my skin-headed friend, you've treated me well or else, just to show my contempt for the whole proceedings, I'd begin to wipe up the hold with you."

The Shaul said, "There's a Kudthu guard within call if I needed one. Probably I would not."

"We have a difference of opinion," said Paddy. "Well then, a friendly little bout to decide the issue. One throw, catch-as-catch-can, just for the sport of it, with no eye-gouging, no skin or hair pulling, I've shaved my whiskers and shed my dirt and I'm a new man."

"As you wish," said the Shaul with a grin that showed pointed teeth of gray metal.

17

Paddy advanced, laid a hand on the Shaul's arm. The Shaul slid away like a greased eel, clasped with corded arms, twisted, Paddy's legs sagged under an unfamiliar leverage. He resisted an instant, then gave, flung himself headlong, gathered his feet below him, heaved and the Shaul tumbled to the deck. Paddy was on him, had his back to the floor. Eye to eye they stared, Paddy's gray-yellow eyes, the Shaul's bright orbs.

Then Paddy jumped up and the Shaul arose, half-sullenly.

"Ah, we're still men on Earth!" crowed Paddy. "You skin-heads can do the square roots, I'll grant you, but for the good side-man in a rough-and-tumble give me one from green old Mother Earth!"

The Shaul gathered up the old clothing, the breakfast dishes, turned to look at Paddy. "Amazing," he said. "An amazing race, you Earthers." He departed, the door closed behind him.

Paddy frowned, bit his lip. "Now just how did he mean that?"

An hour later the Shaul returned, beckoned. "This way, Earther."

Paddy shrugged, obeyed. Behind him a silent Kudthu fell in, ambled along at his heels.

There was excitement aboard the ship. Paddy sensed it from the vibration of skin flaps of the various Shauls in the passages, the staccato burst of conversation, the nervous flickering of long fingers. Peering through a porthole he saw black space and far off a spatter of stars.

About a mile distant hung a great ship with a gray and blue medallion, the ship of the Koton Son. Outside, close against the hull a small clear-domed boat came gliding, coasted to the entrance plug. The

Kudthu pushed at the back of Paddy's head. "Forward, Earther."

Paddy turned, growled. The Kudthu took a step forward, loomed over him. Paddy moved to keep from being trampled.

At the entrance deck a row of Shauls stood with skin flaps distended, rigid as sails, eyes gleaming like tiny light bulbs.

The Kudthu clamped a great hand on Paddy's shoulder. "Stand back. Silence. Be reverent. The Shaul Son of Langtry."

The stillness reminded Paddy of the thick silence of a church during prayer. Then there came a rustle of cloth. An old Shaul with a withered cowl strode down the corridor. He wore a tunic of white cloth, a cuirass enamelled with the scarlet-and-black medallion of Shaul. Looking neither right nor left he stepped through the port out into the crystal-domed boat. The port snapped shut with the suck of escaping air. The boat departed in a flicker of glass and metal. Twenty minutes passed without sound or movement. Paddy fidgeted, stretched, scratched his head.

A hiss, a scrape—and the port opened again. The Kudthu pushed Paddy. "Enter."

Paddy, given no choice, found himself in the space car, which was piloted by a Shaul in a black uniform. Two Kudthu guards followed him into the boat. The port was closed, the boat drifted off into the black gulf, away from the bright heavy side of the ship.

"Now's the time," thought Paddy. "Knock out the two guards, throttle the pilot." He hunched forward, knotted the muscles of his back for a spring. Two great grey hands folded down his shoulders, clamping him on the seat. Paddy, turning his head, saw the blue satin puffballs, which were the eyes of the Kudthu guard, regarding him with suspicion. Paddy relaxed, looked off through the crystal dome.

He saw the Shaul ship a mile distant, then slightly farther out the Badau ship, with a blue and green medallion, amidships—at various distances three other hulls. Dead ahead lay a tiny asteroid, lit along one surface by a high circle of luminous tube.

The boat landed on the asteroid, the port opened. Paddy, expecting the boat's air to rush out into airless space, tensed, gasped, made a warning gesture. Nothing of the sort occurred. There seemed to be an equal pressure of air outside.

The Kudthu thrust him out. He found himself walking to normal gravity though the asteroid, a rock the shape of a man's foot, was hardly two hundred feet across its longest diameter. A gravity unit must be operating, surmised Paddy—somewhere on the underside of the rock.

Below the circle of bright tubing a floor of polished granite flags had been laid with a pattern of baroque pentagons inlaid in gold surrounding a large central star of bright red coral or cinnabar. Five heavy chairs faced inward toward a circular-cockpit three feet in diameter, a foot deep.

The Shaul pilot said to Paddy, "Come." The Kudthu guards shoved. He set out angrily after the Shaul, followed him up onto the brightly lit circular platform and to the central cockpit.

"Step down."

Paddy hesitated, gingerly looking into the opening. The Kudthu pushed him—willy-nilly he stepped down. The Shaul stooped, there came the rattle of chain, a clank and a band encircled Paddy's ankle.

The Shaul said in a hurried voice, "You occupy a very exalted position. See that you bear yourself with respect. When one of the Sons speaks repeat his words in the appropriate language to each of the other Sons—in clockwise order away from the speaker.

"Suppose the Shaul Son who sits in the chair yonder speaks, repeat his words first in Loristanese to the Son there"—he pointed—"then in Koton to the Son from Koto, then in Badaic to the Badau Son and in Pherasic to the Son from Alpheratz A. Do you understand?"

"Very well," said Paddy. "That much of it. What I wish to know is, after I complete my services, what then?"

The Shaul turned half away. "Never mind about that. I can assure you of unpleasantness if you conduct yourself improperly. We Shauls do not torture but the Eagles and the Kotons have no scruples whatever."

"None at all indeed," said Paddy with conviction. "I went to Montras on Koto to a public torturing and the blood-letting quite turned me against the devils. There's a city of hell, that Montras."

"Conduct yourself well, then," the Shaul told him. "They are more than ordinarily irascible, these five Sons. Speak loudly, correctly and mind you, clockwise from the speaker, so there will be the most complete equality of place."

He sprang away from Paddy, ran to the boat and the Kudthu guards lumbered after him.

Alone on the tiny world Paddy searched the sky to see what had occasioned the haste. The five ships, about two miles distant, had drifted together into a roughly parallel formation with their keels toward Paddy.

It was a rather solemn sensation, alone and manacled to this bit of nameless rock, exposed like a victim

on an altar. Paddy bent to examine his bonds. From
the band clamped about his ankle a chain led to a
staple in the stone. He tested it, heaving till the skin
of his hands tore and his stomach muscles knotted,
to no effect.

He stood erect once more, studied his surroundings. There was no bar within reach he might use as
a lever, no fragment of rock to pound with. He was
completely alone, unless someone was stationed on
the far side of the little space-island. Craning his
neck, he saw a concrete casement and a flight of steps
leading down into the rock. Toward the gravity unit,
thought Paddy, and maybe an air generator.

He heard a swish, a drone. He looked up to see a
shining space-boat settling almost at his head. It
touched the surface, the dome swung back. The five
Sons of Langtry stepped out. Silently in a formal line
they advanced to the platform, the gaunt Eagle of
Alpheratz A at one end, then the butter-colored
Loristanese with the flickering features, the Shaul
with the mottled cowl, the saucer-eyed Koton and last
the stocky Badau with the short legs and hump-head.

Paddy watched them approaching with hands
on hips and a curled lip. He shook his head. "And
to think their grandsires were all decent Earthers
such as me. See 'em now, like the menagerie in
Kensington Gardens."

From the rear of the boat came two others, giant
Kudthus. By their purple skins Paddy knew them for
the desexed nearly mindless creatures produced by
surgery and forced feeding. Huge muscular creatures
they were with tumescent red wattles like cocks.

They had been lobotomized to centralize their con-
centration and they moved like creatures in a hyp-
notic state. They took up posts at opposite ends of the

asteroid, where they stood gigantic, quiet, blue puff-ball eyes fixed on Paddy.

The Sons of Langtry separated, took their seats. The Loristanese glanced at Paddy.

"An Earther this year," he observed cheerfully. "Occasionally they're good linguists. They and the Shauls make the best, I believe. But there are few Shaul criminals. I wonder what this rascal's done."

Paddy cocked his head, squinted balefully. Then deciding that his duties had begun, he bowed to the Koton, repeated the words in Koton tongue, did likewise for the Badau, the Eagle and the Shaul. In the final sentence however at the word "rascal" he substituted the Koton word *zhaktum*, equivalent to "reckless fellow"—the Badaic *luad*, meaning "well-appointed knight" in the Robin Hood tradition—the Pherasic *a-kao-up*, meaning "swift flyer;" the Shaul *condosiir*, derived from the old Tuscan *codottiere*.

Then he waited solemnly, politely, for further words. The Loristanese brushed him with a swift glance and a muscle quivered on the yellow jowl but he made no comment.

The Alpheratz Eagle spoke. "There is little to concern us at this meeting. I have observed no noticeable fluctuation in trade volumes, and I see no need for military expansion. Last year's quotas should serve as well."

Paddy translated around the circle. There was a general attitude of agreement.

The Badau said, "I have several petitions to be considered. First from Canopus Four—they want four drives for the purpose of transporting supplies and produce to and from one of their moons which they are using as a cattle range."

The Shaul said, "I have a similar petition. My

agents report that of their allotted sixteen drives they have destroyed five, presumably through experimentation in their laboratories attempting to discover the manifolding process. I speak against the request."

After a few further remarks the petition was denied.

The Badau said, "The second is from a private individual, a non-anthropoid of the Neonomian type. He proposes to circumnavigate space. His plan is to seal himself in a ship, set forth and continue as far and as fast as possible until either he returns or dies."

The petition was granted as being an interesting experiment and not likely to disturb the trade balances.

The Badau looked back to his notes. "Third, a petition from Earth. The natives request a hundred more units."

"A *hundred!*" barked the Koton.

The Shaul leaned back in his chair, grinned. "They have retreated slightly from their previous position. If I recall, for the last fifty years they have demanded unlimited access to the production."

"Slowly they are acquiring a sense of the realities," rumbled the Badau.

The Loristanese said, "There has been only a small rise in the index. I believe one of their units was destroyed in a wreck. Four or five units have deteriorated to the point of uselessness. If we replace those particular units I see little reason for further concessions."

Paddy licked his lips, translated to the Koton: "A small rise in the trade index has occurred. One of their units was destroyed in a wreck, five units have become useless. After replacing these units I see some slight reason for further concessions."

The Koton squared in his seat, turned his saucer eyes at Paddy. Paddy sucked in his breath. "Careful, lad," he told himself. "You're not dealing with the ignorant guards now." He turned to Badau, aware of the Koton's cool stare.

"There has been only a slight rise in the trade index," said Paddy in Badaic. "They wrecked one unit, four others were deteriorated. If we replace these I see no reason for further concessions." And Paddy relaxed as the Koton turned his saucer eyes elsewhere. "A cold clammy feeling it gives a man," thought Paddy. "And they're the ones that invented the nerve-suit, the big-eyed devils."

He finished the round of translations carefully. After a slight pause the votes came in against the Earth petition.

Three other petitions were voted upon. Then the five sat in a rather lengthy silence, ruminatively eyeing Paddy. Bathed in the full flood of soft white light he felt naked and exposed. "Here I am," he muttered disgustedly. "Paddy Blackthorn, late of Skibbereen, County Cork, like a cod on a block. It's the smallest slab of rock in the universe I'm tied to with five unlikely creatures all fixing on the best way to serve up my corpse."

He looked up into the sky. The five ships hung parallel a few miles distant. "It's now time that the Holy Lord was reaching out to look after his own and I've been a good candle-burning Irishman my long life through."

The Shaul said, "Is there any suggestion as to new security regulations?"

The Eagle replied slowly, "A large voice on my planet favors wider dissemination of the secrets, or at least a public repository on each planet known to a responsible group. The Argument, as always, assumes that a catastrophe wipes out the five of us simultaneously, whereupon the technique of manifolding space-drive would be lost."

The Koton said, "And as always the counter-argument is that five minds for one secret is already four more than necessary. A public repository could be looted by a sudden raid. Members of a committee could be kidnapped. Soon there would no longer be a secret. Space would be as full of ships as the Bathcani Sea is of redworms."

The Badau stroked his lump of a head. "My position as always has been that the smaller the extent of critical knowledge, the better. And even if we were all killed the Bank of Loristan would make the hiding places of the data known to our successors."

"Only after ten years," the Eagle said dourly. "Ten years of doubt and confusion."

"Perhaps," said the Shaul easily, "we could make public proclamation to the effect that in the event of catastrophe, the secret would automatically come to light. We need not mention the lapse of ten years, as that would focus attention on the Bank of Loristan. It's popular knowledge that ten years is the period of grace on unrenewed safe deposit boxes."

The Koton said sourly, "Why not entrust the data itself to the Bank of Loristan?"

The Shaul grinned. "There are several reasons why this would not be desirable. Assume this hypothetical catastrophe. Ten years and the mechanism of the Bank automatically ejects the lapsed boxes. There, before the eyes of a clerk, is the secret of space-drive. Secondly—"

"Your first reason is sufficient," said the Koton. "Perhaps the present system is the best."

"The mutual duplication of data protects us against loss of any one set," the Loristanese pointed out, "and the splitting of the secret guarantees a continuance of our mutual dependence."

The Shaul said abruptly, "Now as to the allocation for the five commercial units, eight hundred boat installations..."

One by one the Sons announced the needs of their worlds, and the total moved the Koton to grumble, "We shall be occupied three weeks on Akhabats activating the tubes."

"That is the function of our office," the Loristanese remarked.

"We'll be a week building a new manifold," said the Koton. "Some rascal of an Earther actually tunneled up into the ship, mark you. The fool threw the power switch and Akhabats is safe only because the main gang-bar had been removed for replating."

The Loristanese shrugged, and his fat yellow jowls bounced. "Naturally the dials had been twisted. What could the idiot hope to achieve?"

The Eagle said, "The way of an Earther's mind is past conjecture."

The Shaul made an impatient motion. "Is there any further question as to schedules? If not—"

"We have completed our business," stated the Badau heavily. "Let us make the exchange and depart." He unstrapped a thin band from his wrist, passed it to the Eagle on his left, who in turn handed a similar band to the Shaul, who gave his to the Loristanese, who passed his to the Koton, who passed a band to the Badau.

The Badau grunted in satisfaction. "We are finished for another year, save for the month of toil on Akhabats."

Paddy made himself as inconspicuous as is possible for a man chained to the middle of a brightly-lit stone platform. They might be so engrossed in their talk as to leave him alone on the little world—which in any case would be equivalent to death, he thought glumly.

If the gravity unit were turned off, the air would puff off into the vacuum of space and he would strangle, blow up with the bends. No such luck, in any event. He felt the Koton's saucer eyes upon him as the five arose. The Koton motioned to the guards.

The Koton said, "Remove the prisoner from the platform. Execute him."

Paddy said quizzically, "Would you like that translated, my Lord Koton?"

The Koton ignored him. Paddy watched the Kudthus approaching, purple-skinned giants in black leather uniforms. Either one would make three of him. Here came his death, thought Paddy. How would it be? By bullet—by the heavy Kudthu knives hanging at their belts—by the mere wringing of his neck in the big slab hands?

They towered over him with no more malice or hostility than a farmer selecting a chicken for the pot. One stooped with a key, fumbled at his chains, while the other took a grip on Paddy's shoulder. Paddy's heart was thudding, his throat was thick with sour-tasting fear. It was sad to die at the hands of strange careless things so far from Mother Earth.

III

His leg was free. Paddy in a desperate spasm sank to his knees, bit at the big Kudthu hand, grabbed the knife from the belt of the kneeling Kudthu, hacked at the other's legs. The grip loosened. Paddy broke free, sprang like a rabbit down from the platform. The Shaul brought forth a small hand—weapon, sighted, fired. Paddy veered and the shaft of flickering blue ions cut past his ear.

The Kudthus came lumbering after him, big faces without expression. Another shaft of radiation sizzled past him and he dodged frantically. His mind ran wild. He'd run and run and run to the end of the world. The end of the world was close. Where then? The space-boat? No, the Shaul stood near with his weapon. Where to go? Around the other side? They'd hunt him down.

The concrete casement yawned at his feet, a dim-lit gap. There it was, a bolthole, where at least he could put his back to the wall, where they would not turn their guns for fear of disrupting the gravity....

The gravity! Off with the gravity! Death to himself,

death to all! Would it possibly be unguarded, vulner-
able?

He flung down the steps four at a time, pulled by
the increasingly strong gravitational field. He came to
a little concrete-walled room. A black box ten feet long
was mounted on skids with heavy leads running to a
power bank. Paddy took a deep breath, plodded
across the room, pulled the switch.

The power stopped, the field whisked off into noth-
ingness. Paddy was weightless. Air puffed off into
space at eleven hundred feet a second. A tremendous
force pushed out Paddy's chest as if by an explosion
inside him. Breath gushed up his throat, spewed out
his mouth and he felt a quick distension in his legs,
his arms, felt his ears pounding, his eyes bulging.

He tottered to the switch, threw it back to full
gravity. He was master on this little world, lord of
life and death. Too late, he thought numbly—useless. The air had departed at the speed of sound
and faster. It would return only at gravitational
acceleration.

The vacuum would be nearly complete for an hour
yet, while all on the little world died. But no—he felt
the tingling at his skin slowly diminish, the throb of
his throat lessen. He opened his mouth, gasped. Air—
air in the little room at least, very rare yet, seepage
from cracks, a film held by molecular attraction and
the gravity of the asteroid itself, now concentrated
around the gravity unit.

Paddy dragged himself up the stairs against the
gravity, augmented as it was by his nearness to the
unit. As he climbed he felt the atmosphere rapidly
thinning. His head pounded in a near-vacuum as
he peered over the casement. The Kudthus lay
sprawled twenty feet distant in the dark pool of

their hemorrhages. The five Sons of Langtry lay dead in a little clump around the boat. Paddy, blinked, taken aback.

The most appalling crime in the history of space had been committed. Genocide, defilement of holy places, treachery against the entire universe—no sin could rival his deed. The Five Sons dead by his hand!

Paddy licked his puffed lips. It seemed a great-to-do for the mere pulling of a switch. They would have killed him without glancing to see whether his way was to kick or to twitch. He looked across the platform at the boat, stared past the luminous tubing at the five ships.

They lay in a quiet parallel rank. Ha, could not the fools sense the horror? Or their telescopes must tell them something was amiss. Of course they might be under orders to keep eyes away from instruments for fear that there might be lip-reading.

Paddy looked back to the boat with the longing of a lover. His sight was blurring pink, blood was running from his nose. The hundred feet to the boat was like a thousand miles. Two feet above the concrete casement meant strangulation. He backed down the shaft to breathe and gather his wits.

He considered. How would the gravity unit be turned off? By someone in a pressure suit, to escape his own doom. Would there be such a garment left at hand for the purpose? He found it hanging in the shadows behind the powerbank, and was into it with what speed he could provoke from his trembling fingers.

He fitted the dome over his head, turned on the air. Ah-h-h, what a blessed thing was the pure thick air with a taste like the finest water.

But no time to savor his air. Up—if he wished to

escape the nerve-suit. He sprang up the steps, darted across the dead world. At the corpses of the five Sons of Langtry he stopped short. Around the Shaul's thin forearm he found a glint of gold, unclasped the band. Then to the Koton, the leathery Badau, the Eagle and the butter-yellow Loristanese.

Jingling the five bands Paddy ran to the ship. Inside the port, throw home the dogs, to the pilot's seat. He groped among the controls until he found the lift valve. Inching it open he raised the ship a trifle above the surface, slewed it slowly around to the opposite side of the world.

Then, keeping the little asteroid between himself and the five ships as long as possible he turned the accelerator on full and the little ship fell out, out out—into the deep well of space with stars flickering the shiny pebbles at the bottom.

Now—on with the space-drive and he was safe. *Safe!*

He slumped back into the seat, fell into a torpor....

Paddy looked about his ship, letting the sight of glossy metal and glass, the fittings, fabrics, the exquisite equipment gladden his vision, luxuriating in the surroundings like a gourmet rolling the flavor of a fine sauce through his mouth.

Paddy rose from the couch, stretched like one reborn. The boat was a new life, a symbol of rebirth. His past seemed remote as if only a tenuous wisp linked Paddy Blackthorn of the Akhabats jail and Paddy Blackthorn standing on the deck-covering of crisp scarlet eggshell pile.

Paddy clapped his arms to his sides, grinned with honest joy. Not only was he free with his life—enough to rejoice about—but he had played a devastating joke on his would-be slayers. A magnificent joke to make his name one for history. It was the pattern of the circumstances that exactly filled a socket in the human brain, the biter bit, the bully tripped up by the underdog in a gutter full of slops.

Paddy strolled here and there, surveyed his prize. It seemed to be engineered less for cruising than for use as an interplanetary pleasure boat. It carried no large supply of stores, no arsenal.

The fittings were of a quality and precision befitting the ceremonial boat of the Sons of Langtry. The joinerwork was a rare wood from a far planet, showing a grain of black and golden-green. There was a brown-violet matanne upholstery on the couch and the scarlet carpet with the pile that was like stepping on candied rose-petals.

Paddy returned to the pilot's platform, studied the astrogation instruments. A boat of this type, with no cost spared on its construction would embody new equipment, much of which might be unfamiliar to him. And as he glanced along the panel he found levers, dials, arms, whose use he did not comprehend. He left them untouched. For all he knew one might set off an emergency SOS call.

He turned to the wide couch, inspected the shiny heap of his loot—five bands of gold, each with a thin square compartment. Paddy stood back with a sensation close to awe. "Here," he said, "is the treasure of the ages, which all the wealth of Earth would buy cheap....And it's me, Paddy Blackthorn, who handles these lovelies.

"But now let's open them and we'll see how to curl space-drive into them shiny tubes so next time there won't be that great explosion...."

He snapped off the lid of the first, withdrew a bit

of stiff parchment. It was imprinted with heavy Badaic letters:

The Kamborogian Arrowhead Suite 10
The Foolish Man's Inclination Page 100

Paddy raised his eyebrows high. "And what's this?" He was thunderstruck, apprehensive. Was there some colossal error?

"Ah, well," said Paddy, "now we'll see." He opened the second band.

Like the first it contained a bit of parchment, written in Pherasic script which Paddy could not read. He passed on to the third, which was stamped with the neat Shaul cuneiform:

Corescens, the black wall.
Three up, two over
Irradiate with angstroms 685, 1444, 2590, 3001
Photograph.

Paddy groaned, opened the fourth band. It held a key, engraved with the Loristanese loops and lines, nothing more. Paddy tossed it aside.

The parchment in the Koton band read:

The Plain of Thish, where Arma-Geth
shows the heroes to the wondering stars.
Under my mighty right hand.

Paddy flung himself back on the couch. "A bloody treasure hunt, that's what!" he cried. "And to think I've risked all for the only clues. Well, then, by Fergus, I'll fling them from the port and have done with it!"

But he folded the four parchment slips carefully around the key, and replaced them in one of the bands, which he fitted on his own wrist.

"Now for home," thought Paddy. "Peace and quiet and no more of this space-rampaging—and yet—" He rubbed his chin dubiously. He was by no means safe. He had escaped the asteroid with his skin, but the Langtry swarmed space with wasps in a shed.

He was safe from the rear. But was he safe from interception? Space-wave messages flew as swiftly as thought. The description of the boat and Paddy's personal coordinates would reach every outpost in space. Paddy would be the quarry of the universe. Ordinary misdeeds would go unchallenged while the authorities combed the worlds for Paddy Blackthorn.

Exultation waned to fretful uneasiness. In his mind's-eye he saw the placards, tacked up in every saloon, every post office, every transportation agency in the known universe—displaying his picture and the caption—

WANTED—*for interplanetary crime!*
Paddy Blackthorn, Earther. *Dangerous!*
Height, six feet; weight, one hundred eighty
pounds. Age, approximately thirty. Red-
brown hair, hazel eyes, broken nose.

"And then," grumbled Paddy, "there'll be my fingerprints, my tongueprint, my psychograph. They'll describe the hairs of my head and they'll write at the bottom, 'Catch this fiend and name your own reward.' I'm cursed with the luck of the devil himself. There's no haven for me on Earth, no place for me but the Thieves' Cluster—and then how long?"

He rummaged through the chart index, found the proper code, punched the buttons and in front of him, projected by a series of lenses, appeared the sphere of space surrounding the Thieves' Cluster.

At the edge a blue gleam of light indicated his own position with a white arrow indicating the vector of his position and course. Paddy sighted, gingerly changed course until the vector pointed at the Thieves' Cluster.

He turned on the space-wave. It was staccato with coded messages. Let 'em rave, thought Paddy. Once in the Thieves' Cluster, not even the Sons of Langtry could drag him forth. Of course they might send agents in to assassinate him. But would they? He was the only man alive who knew, if not the secret of space-drive, the whereabouts of the secret.

IV

The Thieves' Cluster was a group of eight suns in the Perseian Limbo which had picked up a jostling swarm of dark stars, planets, planetoids, asteroids, meteorites, and general debris. Here was end-haven for the lost men of the worlds. Among the hundred thousand satellites a man could dodge a low-boat like a rabbit ducking a dog in a mile of blackberry thicket.

If he cared nothing for the life of the settled planets, if he had money to pay for his stores, if he could protect himself, then he could live his life among the jostling little worlds with small fear of civilized justice.

There was no law in the Thieves' Cluster except at Eleanor on the central planet Spade-Ace. Here a government of sorts existed—an order of men forced to cooperate by fear and despair, a society of the antisocial. The executive committee of the government was the Blue-nose Gang, after Blue-nose Pete, mayor of Eleanor.

At Eleanor the strictest law in the universe was enforced. If a man could win to the Eleanor space-field he could sleep in an alley with his loot on his

37

chest and when he awoke his gold would be there. The apparatus was clumsy and harsh but if a man violated the law of Eleanor the Gang would have his life.

Paddy slipped through the crush of flaming suns and bright worlds without hindrance, fell against the swampy side of Spade-Ace, leveled off, flew screaming a few miles above the reed-covered morass. A ridge of black rock rose at the horizon. He crossed it and below him was Eleanor, a spatter of white and brown at the base of the mountain.

He dropped to the field beside the alteration docks, where a Badau double-monitor lay half-dismantled.

He jumped out of the domed boat, ran across the field to the line of ships at the boundary. At a hydrant he flung himself down, turned on the water, drank, drank, drank.

An Earther lounging nearby, a tall dark man with narrow yellow eyes, watched him curiously. "Run out of water, Red?"

Paddy pulled himself to his feet, ran his wet hands across his face.

"Faith, I've eaten shrimp preserved in sweet syrup now it's four days and vile fare it is, believe me, after the third bite."

"Sounds rough," said the tall dark man. He nodded at the boat. "Nice rig you're flying. Planning to sell or holding on to her?"

Paddy leaned against the hangar. "Perhaps you'd spare a cigarette? Thanks." He blew out a great puff of smoke. "Now as to the ship, as I am without funds, I think she'll have to be sold. What might a boat like that bring?"

The Earther squinted reflectively. "A hundred thousand, maybe a little more. Say a hundred thirty."

Paddy rubbed his face, already red-bearded. "Hmmm. The drive alone is worth a million on Earth."

"This ain't Earth, Red."

"If what I hear of prices here in the cluster is so, that'll feed me about a month."

The Earther laughed. "Not quite that bad. Depends on what kind of service you like. The Casino Lodge up Napoleon Street is high. If you want something cheaper, try the Bowsprit, down Pickpocket Alley. It's clean but not too stylish."

Paddy thanked the man gravely. "And perhaps you can tell me the best place to sell the boat because in truth I haven't a cent in my pocket."

The tall man pointed across the field. "If you want a quick deal to go in that door with the yellow glass. Tell the Canope girl you want to talk to Ike."

Paddy drove a hard bargain, eloquently describing the luxury, the comfort, the appointments of the space-boat.

"—the former property of one of the highest lords of Shaul! Like his private boudoir! Marvelous, my friend Ike, and the anti-gravs overpowered so that you never know when you leave the ground...."

He left the space-field with a hundred and forty-five thousand marks in assorted notes—yellow, blue, and blue-green. He turned a district of warehouses, second-hand shops, rooming-houses. Then, climbing a slight rise, he came to the quarter of the restaurants, taverns, bordellos.

Farther up the hill were the concrete and glass hotels, catering to exiles and regular visitors— smugglers, blackbirders, ship-stealers, spies. The city was crowded, the streets filled with sauntering men of all races and variants—first-stage types like the Canopes, Maeves, Dyoks, varying in only a few details, then along the metamorphological gamut. The Shauls and Kotons, Labirites and Green-Rassins and then the Alpheratz Eagles, gaunt, sharp, bony as herons, the elfin Asmasians, the fat butter-yellow Loristanese.

Paddy ate a slow meal at an Earth-style restaurant, then crossed the street to a barber shop, where he bought a shave and a haircut. At a clothing store he dressed himself in clean underclothes, a somber blue jumper, soft boots.

The proprietress was an ancient Loristanese woman, whose youthful yellow had darkened to a horse-chestnut color. As Paddy paid, he leaned confidentially across the counter, winked.

"And where might I find a good beauty shop, my knowledgeable charmer?"

The old woman gave him his change and the directions together. "Upstairs and down the hall. The doctor gives you a new face as easy as I change your clothes."

Upstairs walked Paddy, down a long corridor broken by a line of cheap wooden doors, each door bearing a nameplate: Galtee Stowage—Chiutt Explosive Supply—Pretagni and Dha, Loristanese Financial Consultants—Ramadh Singh, Funeral Consultant and Insurance, Corpses Buried Anywhere—Dr. Ira Tallogg, Dermatologist.

Three hours later Paddy was a different man. His hair was black with Optichrome B. No longer was his nose broken. Instead it resembled the nose Paddy had worn during his youth. Even his fingers had been capped with new prints and his tongue had been slightly stitched, changing his voice and altering the pattern of the surface.

Paddy surveyed the new man in the full-length

mirror. Behind him the doctor stood silently—a fat neatly-shaven Earther with a sour expression.

Paddy turned. "How much, doctor?"

"Five thousand marks."

As Paddy counted out the money it came as a sudden sharp discovery that the doctor was the sole link between the old and the new. He said, "How much for the operation and how much for keeping your mouth shut?"

The doctor said, "All of it either way. I don't talk. I get asked plenty. There're more spies in Eleanor than there is in Novo Mundo. All I need to do is talk once and I'm done. The Blue-nose Gang would get me inside the day."

Paddy studied his new profile. "Would you talk for a million marks and a free ride to Earth?"

The doctor replied warily, "Hard to say. Nobody's ever offered it to me."

Paddy tilted his head, looked down his nose at the foreshortened reflection. The doctor connected the red-headed fugitive from Akhabats and the dark man from nowhere like the equal sign of an equation. As he had pointed out, Eleanor swarmed with spies.

Now if he, Paddy Blackthorn, were the Executive Intelligencer on one of the Langtry worlds he would station a man at the Eleanor space-field—maybe leaning against the hangar. A man landing a ship with a crystal dome would set many wheels in motion.

They would know he had bought a blue jumper before he appeared again on the streets. They might learn that he had visited the doctor. So far his new appearance was unknown. He was still nameless. So long as he was unknown and nameless he was safe in the crowds of the wordless gray men coming and going.

The doctor was the link. He would be approached, questioned, offered enormous bribes, an all-embracing pardon for past sins.

"Doc," said Paddy gently, "do you have a back door out of here?"

The doctor looked up from putting away his tools. "Fire escape down the rear," he said shortly.

It would be watched, thought Paddy. He eyed the doctor speculatively. He could trust nobody. What was a million, ten million, a hundred million marks, one way or the other, either to himself or the Langtry worlds? The wealth of the universe, the cycle of empire was clasped to his wrist.

He should kill the doctor. He should but he could not. The doctor read the thought in his eyes, drew back, read the dismissal, relaxed. Others had looked at him with the same expression and for that reason he carried a gun in his pocket.

Paddy went to the window, looked out into a drab back alley. Across the street was a blank wall streaked with grime, raddled with a native red fungus.

Paddy felt trapped. They knew where he was. Any minute he could expect a bullet in his head or kidnapping and the nerve-suit—a lifetime in the nerve-suit. His flesh crawled. It was a mistake, landing on Spade-Ace. As soon as he had set foot on the planet, his presence had been reported. Langtry agents would be converging like hounds on a fox.

And yet he had to land sometime, somewhere. Paddy thought of the shrimps in syrup, grimaced. No water, no food—Earth would have been little, if any, better. He would have been extradited from Earth almost as soon as he landed and his story laughed off by a bribed magistrate.

He turned back from the window, surveyed the

dim little room with its settee and spindly blue lethepl-
ant, the operating table and racks of instruments,
cabinets full of bottles. The walls were cheap spraywood, the ceiling the same.

Paddy turned to the door. "Now I'm going, Doc,
and never forget—I'll know if you spill and you'll sore
regret it."

The doctor seemed to take no offense, having
heard the same threat from each of his patients. He
nodded matter-of-factly and Paddy took his leave. The
door latched behind him.

Paddy looked up and down the empty corridor.
It smelled of sour varnish, of corners full of dust.
Next door to the doctor was the office of Ramadh
Singh, Funeral Consultant. Paddy laid his ear to
the glass panel in the door. It was late in the afternoon. The office seemed to be empty. Paddy tried
the door—locked.

Again he looked up and down the corridor. On
Earth there would be no hesitation. One Spade-Ace a
card cheat was hung head downward, his ankles
nailed to a high beam. A burglar was shot on apprehension.

Paddy muttered, "The lure of gold is leading me
to the edge of crime." Setting his shoulder to the
glass he heaved. The glass bent out of the molding.
Paddy reached in, snapped the latch, slid open the
door, entered.

The office was a mere cubicle, equipped with a
desk, a table displaying miniature coffins and urns at
various prices, a small mnemiphot, a battered screen.
On the wall hung a calendar and a group photograph
of a family standing in front of a small frame cottage,
evidently on Earth.

Paddy crossed the room, put his ear to the partition. On the other side he could hear a scrape of motion—the doctor setting his office to rights.

To Paddy's right was a little closet. He looked in, saw a tank of mist-cleaner, a medicine closet built into the partition. Opening the door of the medicine closet and pulling out Ramadh Singh's various unguents, incenses, lotions, Paddy had only a thin layer of spraywood between himself and the doctor's office.

Now, thought Paddy, we'll see, we'll see. If I've been followed, presently they'll be curious and come on up to see where I am. If they come up and question the doctor I'll know the worst, and be prepared.

He heard voices, bent his ear to the cabinet. The doctor had a patient—a rough voice like an Asmasian. He was suffering from heat rash and the doctor gave him a package of sal-negative. Another patient, suffering from ionic burns, was treated.

There was a wait of twenty minutes, then another patient, then another twenty minutes—and now a fresh new voice with a different timbre. Paddy cocked his ear. The voice was feminine, full of soft round overtones. The woman asked, "Are you Dr. Tallogg?"

There was a pause. Paddy pictured the doctor's slow sour scrutiny. "That's right."

"Dr. Tallogg," said the woman's voice, "you know that your brother, Dr. Clement Tallogg, is looking for you?"

There was a long silence. Finally, in a dim muffled voice, "I have no brother. What do you want?"

"I want to pay you five hundred thousand marks. That's half a million marks." She paused to let the figure sink in. "I want to take you back to Paris. We can leave in fifteen minutes. When we arrive you'll find that your brother is no longer interested in your whereabouts, that a certain set of books has been found. I can arrange all this. All I want in return is some information."

Another long pause and Paddy's eyes narrowed. Sweat poured down his ribs. What temptation to put before a man! Home, wealth, the sweet milk of friendship—how could he resist? He would *not* resist.

"What kind of information?" came the low dim voice.

"A tall red-haired man about thirty years old entered the building, came to your office. He has not been seen to leave. Very probably you have altered his appearance, possibly provided him with an unobtrusive route to the streets. What I want is an exact description of this man, his new appearance, his new coordinates and what you know of his future plans."

The silence was of a full minute's duration and Paddy held his breath.

"Show me the money."

There was a soft thud, a click, a slap. "Right there."

"And—the other matters?"

"You'll have to accept my word."

The doctor made a soft sound of scornful rejection. Silence.

"Here," said the doctor. "Swallow this."

Hesitation.

"What is it?"

"It's one of the Asmasian ordeal drugs. If an antidote is taken inside of half an hour no harm of any sort will result. If not you will die in some pain. When you put me aboard this boat I'll give you the antidote."

The woman laughed. "By a curious coincidence I likewise carry with me a quantity of the ordeal poison. If you will take my dose I'll take yours—and we're both protected.

"Fair enough."

There were sounds, a click, another. Then the doctor's voice came, deliberate, slow, detached.

"The red-haired man now is very dark—a Mediterranean type. Here—this is what the prototype looks like. He resembles this very closely. You may keep it. He wears a blue jumper, soft boots. He speaks with a slight accent of some sort—I can't quite place it.

"I know nothing of his past, or his future plans. His fingerprints"—a pause, a rustle of papers—"this is the set I gave him. He left my office about an hour or an hour and a half ago. Where he went I have no idea."

The woman's voice said, "Did you let him out some secret way?"

"No," said the doctor. "There is a door into the cellar and out into the street that no one very much knows about but I did not take him to it. He simply walked out the door and closed it."

The woman said thoughtfully, "He has not been seen to leave."

"Then—" the doctor started. Paddy pulled himself out of the closet, slid open Ramadh Singh's door, slipped out into the hall, stepped to Dr. Tallogg's door, slid it ajar an inch. The drab waiting room was empty. Voices came from the inner room.

The door slid quietly open. Paddy slipped in like a dark dream.

He had no weapon—he must go carefully. He stepped across the room, saw a shoulder in gray-green fabric, a hip in dark green. On the hip hung a pouch. If she carried a weapon it would lie in this pouch.

Paddy stepped through the door, threw an arm around the woman's throat, dipped into her pouch with his right hand. He pulled out an ion gun, pointed it at the doctor.

The doctor had his own weapon in his hand. He held it as if it were very hot, as if he were not sure where to aim it.

Paddy said, "Put down that gun!" in a voice like an iron bell. "Put it down, I say!"

The doctor peered at him with almost comical indecision. Paddy heaved the struggling woman forward, reached, took the gun from Tallogg's numb fingers. He shoved it inside his jumper. The woman sprang clear, turned, faced Paddy, her mouth parted, eyes wide with black wide pupils staring.

"Quiet!" warned Paddy. "I'm a desperate man. I'll shoot if you drive me to it."

"What do you want?" asked Tallogg quietly. He now bore himself with the indifference of a man condemned.

Paddy grinned, a wide toothy grin. "First, doctor, you will conduct me and this lady to the street through your secret way."

The woman stiffened, began to speak, then halted, watching Paddy in frowning calculation.

The doctor said, "Perhaps I will, perhaps I won't." He nodded wearily at the ion gun. "You intend to shoot me anyway."

Paddy shrugged. "I won't shoot. We'll sit here and talk. Faith, I'm a great talker. I'll tell you of the Grand Rally at Skibbereen, I'll talk by the hour of Fionn and Diarmuid. Then there's Miletus and the old heroes." He looked brightly at the doctor. "Now what do you say to that?"

The doctor's mouth had dropped. He said forlornly, "I suppose I lose nothing by talking you out."

Paddy turned to the woman. "And I'll ask you to take me to your boat."

She said, "Now listen to me, Paddy Blackthorn."

He took stock of her. She was younger than he had expected and a great deal smaller. There were few inches more than five feet of her and she was slim to boot. She had a small face, short dark hair clinging close to her head. Except for lustrous dark eyes Paddy thought her rather plain, hardly feminine. His taste was for the long-limbed brown-haired girls of Maeve, laughing light-headed girls.

"I hate killing," muttered Paddy. "Lucky for you it is that I harm never so much as a fly unless first it stings me. Now as for you, walk quiet and calm and there'll be no great harm done to you. But mind—no tricks!"

He motioned to the doctor. "Lead."

The doctor said sourly, "Did I understand you to say that you don't intend to shoot me?"

Paddy snorted. "You understand nothing. Get moving."

The doctor spread out his hands helplessly. "I merely wanted to state that if we are to leave I wish to take along the antidote to the ordeal poison I gave the young woman. If I don't have hers she won't give me mine."

Paddy said, "Give it to me."

The doctor hesitated, eyeing the girl doubtfully.

"If I don't get it I'll sit here till you fall sideways from the poison."

The doctor shuffled to the drawer, tossed Paddy an envelope.

Paddy looked at the girl. "Now yours."

Without a word she tossed him a vial. The doctor's eyes hungrily followed the arc of the flight, riveted on Paddy's arm as he pocketed the drugs.

"Now move," said Paddy blithely. "You're both under death sentences, like me in the brick jail at

Akhabats. Except I was an honest thief. You two are traitors to your old Mother Earth."

The doctor led them along the sour-smelling hall, slowly, hoping for interruption. Paddy said pleasantly, "And if there's trouble, Doc, I'll smash these bottles down on the floor." The doctor's gait lengthened. He opened a narrow door, led them down a flight of damp stones heavy with a musty reek of some nameless Spade-Ace mold.

Two flights down and the stairs opened into the basement below the clothing store, a long low room dug into the ground, lit by antique glow-tubes. Old cases, dusty furniture cast tall black shadows—junk brought across the mindless miles of space to rot and moulder in a basement.

Quietly, sedately, they moved through the basement, forming strange silhouettes against the higgledy-piggledy background. Paddy grinned. They didn't dare attack, they didn't dare run. He had them in a double grip with the gun and the poison.

The doctor glanced at his watch. "Fifteen minutes," he said thickly. "Then the antidote does us no more good." He looked at Paddy with hot eyes, waiting for Paddy to answer.

Paddy motioned silently. The doctor turned, stepped up on a bench, heaved at a slanting door. It swung up and out, letting a slender shaft of white light into the basement. The doctor looked right, left, motioned with a plump arm.

"Come on up, all's clear."

He stepped on up, the woman followed nimbly and then came Paddy, cautiously. They stood at the bottom of a light well, between two buildings, with a slit two feet wide running out to the street.

Paddy said to the girl, "Where is the space-boat?"

"North of town on the dust flat."

"Let's go."

They sidled from between the buildings out into a dark street. The doctor turned to the right, led them among the dismal mud huts of the Asmasian quarter. At a square of light he paused, looked at his watch.

"Ten minutes." He turned to Paddy. "Did you hear me? Ten minutes!"

Paddy waved him on. The door turned and they continued out into the open country in back of the town—a region of open sewers, fields packed with unwanted refuse from a thousand stolen ships. Here and there stood the shack of some creature with habits too disgusting to be tolerated even by the tolerant men of Eleanor.

They came out on a plain of white volcanic dust, dark gray in the planet-spangled night of Spade-Ace, and the town of Eleanor was at their backs—a low unsightly blotch spotted with white and yellow lights.

Paddy searched across the field for the dark shape of the boat. He turned a stormy glance at the woman. The doctor peered at his watch. "About a minute..."

The woman's voice glistened with triumph. "I have a space-boat. It's not here. It's at the main field. You're bluffing, Paddy Blackthorn. You want my space-boat more than I want my life. Now *I'm* making the terms. You've got to go along with me or else kill me."

"And kill you I will," growled Paddy, pulling out his gun.

"And kill yourself at the same time. Langtry agents are pouring into Eleanor by the boatload. They know you're here. They'll get you inside of four hours. You can't hide and you can't get away. I'm your only chance. Cooperate with me, and we both win—and Earth wins. Refuse and we both die—and Earth loses because before they kill you they'll get what they want from you."

Paddy stood limp, angry. "Ah, you scheming, hagwoman, you've got me like Cuchulin's goat. You still have the audacity to claim you serve Earth?"

She smiled in the darkness. "You don't believe me? You've never heard of the Earth Agency?"

The doctor whined, "The antidotes! Hurry, man, or we'll be dead!"

"Come here," growled Paddy. He grabbed the woman, felt for scars that might be left by an amputated skin-flap. "No, you're not Shaul. And sure you're no Eagle, no Badau. You're not white enough for a Koton—not to mention the eyes—and you're not yellow enough for a Loristanese. Of course," he grumbled, "there's little profit in wondering about your race—you might be selling out to any of them."

The woman said, "I work for Earth Agency. It's your last chance. Give me the antidote—or I'll die and you'll die and the Langtry worlds will lord it over the universe for the rest of time. There'll never come another chance like this, Paddy Blackthorn."

"*Quick!*" cried the doctor. "*Quick!* I can feel the—"

Paddy contemptuously tossed them the antidotes. "Go on then. Save your miserable lives, and let me be." He turned on his heel, strode off across the powdery dust.

The woman's voice came to his back. "Wait a minute, Paddy Blackthorn. Don't you want to leave Spade-Ace?"

Paddy said no word, paced on, blind with rage.

Her voice came to him, "I have a space-boat!" She

came running up beside him, panted, "We'll take the secret of the drive to Earth."

Paddy slowed his stride, halted, looked down into her wide dark eyes. He turned, went back to where the doctor stood forlornly. Paddy grasped the doctor by the shoulders.

"Look now, Tallogg. You have your half million that you got selling me out. Buy yourself a boat this very night—this very hour. Leave the planet. If you make it to Earth you can sell the boat and be a rich man. Do you hear?"

"Yes," said Tallogg dully. His shoulders hung as if under a yoke.

"Then go," said Paddy. "And if you love old Earth don't return to your office. Don't go there at all."

The doctor muttered something indistinguishable, became a blot in the gray murk. He was gone.

Paddy looked after him. "Better should I have burnt a hole in him and so saved us much concern for the future."

The woman said, "Never mind that. Let's go and we'll head for Earth."

"Very well." Paddy sighed. "It's not as I had planned it."

"Be glad you're alive," she said. "Now let's go."

By a back route they walked to the space field, quietly crossed to her boat at the far end. Paddy looked at the boat doubtfully from end to end.

"Those are crowded quarters for the pair of us, I'm thinking. Now maybe a decent respectable girl wouldn't care to—"

She snapped, "Never mind that, Paddy Blackthorn. You keep your distance, I'll keep mine—and my reputation can look after itself."

"Yerra," muttered Paddy, "and who'd want to

touch such a spit-cat and plain to boot? Well then—into the boat with you and may be the best man of us win."

As she opened the port the beam of light fell on them. A man's voice said hoarsely. "Just a minute, just a minute."

Paddy put his hand on the girl's back, shoved her in, started after her. "Come back here," said the dark shape and the voice was louder. "I'll shoot!"

Paddy turned, aimed at the light with Dr. Tallogg's gun. His beam struck square. In the spatter of orange and purple flames from the shorted powerpack, Paddy glimpsed the man's face—the narrow-faced narrow-eyed man who had been leaning against the hangar when Paddy dropped down to the space-field. His face was convulsed by pain, surprise, hate, by the shock of the beam. The lamp guttered into a red flicker, died—and the dark shape seemed to slump.

"Quick!" hissed the girl. "There'll be more."

Paddy jumped in. She sealed the port, ran to the pilot's seat, pulled back the power-arm—and the boat rose into the ash-gray sky of Spade-Ace.

V

They rose from the field into the glare of the eight suns strewn around the sky at various distances.

"Watch the field," said the girl, "through the telescope."

Paddy watched. "There's a couple boats taking off."

"Spies." She crouched in the bucket seat, aimed the boat's nose at one of the spots of black space showing between the jostle of the suns, planets, planetoids. "Here we go."

Paddy jerked forward. "Hey—that's dangerous, woman! There's lots of stuff out there!"

He quieted because already the Thieves' Cluster was far behind. For a second, two seconds, they flew—then she cut off the power. A relay clicked, the space-drive bar snapped back, Thieves' Cluster was a lambent blot astern.

She turned the nose another direction, repeated the maneuver. Thieves' Cluster was a bright spot. Once again, off at an odd angle—off with the drive and they were coasting out in inter-star isolation.

The girl left the controls, went to the communicator. Paddy watched her suspiciously. "And now what
might you be doing?"

"I'm calling the Agency—on coded space-waves."
She snapped a switch, tuned down a piercing whistle
that rang through the room. She set five dials, and
now a voice said: "E A...E A...E A..."

The girl spoke into the mesh. "Fay Bursill,
59206...Fay Bursill, 59206."

A minute passed, the voice changed. "Go ahead,
Fay."

"I've got Paddy Blackthorn here in the boat."

"*Good work, Fay!*" There was exultation in the
voice. "Where are you?"

"Oh—roughly Aries 3500 or 4000. Shall I come
home?"

"Lord no, keep away. There's a net of ships around
the system almost nose to nose and they're searching
every hull that comes near. You'd never make it. But
here's what you can do. Have Paddy—"

The voice changed to an ululating howl that jarred
their teeth, clawed at their inner ears. "Turn him off!"
yelled Paddy. "He's talking nonsense!"

Fay flung the switch. The silence was like salve.

"Jammed," said Fay grimly. "They're on the frequency."

Paddy blinked dubiously. "Did they hear what
you said?"

She shook her head. "I don't see how they could.
The code is changed every week. And it's easy to jam
the message."

Paddy said, "We'd better get out of here fast. They
might have us spotted."

Fay threw on the power. She sat silently, face
intent, mouth curved down at the corners. Serious

creature, thought Paddy. Odd, fey—that was her name, Fay. Paddy decided it suited her.

She said frowning, "There's no place for us to go now. They'll be watching every port."

"If we could only have ducked out of Eleanor without being caught at it," muttered Paddy. "Then they wouldn't have known where I was."

"Unless they caught the doctor. And in any event they wouldn't be taking any chances." She looked at him with eyes half-challenging, half-wistful. "Now—may I see it, this space-drive formula that's making so much trouble for me? Maybe we can broadcast it to Earth on the code frequency—or we can find a dead little world and hide it."

Paddy laughed. "Young lady—Miss Bursill—whatever your name—I have no secret to the space-drive."

"*What!*" Her eyes burnt even larger in her small face. "Then why all the turmoil? You *must* have it."

Paddy yawned. "The five Sons trusted no one. Not even their successors, the new Sons, know what it is I've got. No one in the universe knows—except me."

"Well, what is it?" she asked crossly. "Or do you intend to be mysterious?"

Paddy said blandly, "No indeed. I'm surely not the type. Well, for one thing, it's not any directions on how to mix up space-drive. It's a key and four little slips of parchment. And all that's on them is a set of addresses."

She stared at him and plain or not, thought Paddy, she had very lovely eyes, bright and intelligent, and her features weren't as pinched as he first thought but almost chiseled—delicate. Indeed, thought Paddy, he had seen worse-looking wenches. But this one—she was too pale and set, too sexless for his tastes.

"May I see them?" she asked politely.

And why not, thought Paddy. He unsnapped the band.

She stared. "You're carrying them around your wrist?"

"Where else?" demanded Paddy with asperity. "I never intended to be kidnaped and transported by a black imp of a female."

She took the bits of parchment and the key. The first was written in the Pherasic script, which Paddy had been unable to read.

She scrutinized it and he saw her lips moving. "Och, then you can read that heathen scribble?"

"Certainly I can read it. It says: '28.3063 degrees north, 190.9995 degrees west. Under the Sacred Sign.'" She laughed. "It's like a treasure hunt. But why should they write directions down like this?"

Paddy shrugged. "For each other, I gather. In case one of them got killed, then the others would know where the records were hid."

Fay said thoughtfully, "We're not far from Alpheratz."

Paddy stared aghast. "They'd draw and quarter me!" They'd wear out their nerve-suits! They'd—"

She said coolly, "We could be tourists from Earth, making the Langtry Line. Alpheratz A, back into Pegasus for Scheat, down Andromeda—Ddhil, Almach, Mirach. There're thousands of others doing the same thing. A honeymoon couple, that's what we'd be. It's the last place they'd be looking for you. You'd never be safer."

"Not much," said Paddy energetically. "I want to get back to Earth with my life and there I'll sell these bits to whomever wants to buy."

She looked at him disgustedly. "Paddy Blackthorn—*I'm* running this ship. We settled that once."

"Och," cried Paddy, "it's no source of wonder that you've never married. God pity the man who gets such a witch. No man would have you with your insistent ways."

Fay smiled wryly. "No? Are you so sure, Paddy Blackthorn?"

Paddy said, "Well, it's sure that I, for one, would never have the taste for the black-headed pint of spite that you are. I'd be drinking whiskey to ease my soul by night and by day."

She sneered. "We're both of us suited then. And now—Alpheratz A."

From Alpheratz A to Alpheratz B the stream of boats was like a caravan of ants—bringing pods, fibers, sheets, crystallized wood, fruit, meal, pollen, oil, plant-pearls, a thousand other products of B's miraculous vegetation to the windy gray world A, returning with agricultural equipment and supplies for the jungle workers.

Into this swarm of space craft Paddy and Fay merged their boat unnoticed.

They dropped toward the bright side of the planet. Fay asked Paddy, "Ever been here before?"

"No, my travels never brought me this far north. And from the looks of the planet, I'd as lief be back on Akhabats. If it's as dry there at least it's a planet with blue water." Paddy gestured at the telescopic projection on the screen. "Now just what might that ocean consist of? Maybe it's mud?"

Fay said, "It's not water. It's something like a gas. It has all the properties of a gas except that it won't mix with air. It's heavier and settles out in the low places like water or fog—and the air rests on top."

"Indeed, now—and is it poison?"

She turned him a side-glance. "If you fall in you smother, because there's no oxygen."

"Then that will be a fine place to leave our boat. And chance being good, we might find it another time."

"We'd better stick to our first plan. We'll be less conspicuous."

"And suppose they recognize Paddy Blackthorn and his black-headed mistress—ah, now, don't take me wrong. That's just what they'd be calling you and no thanks to them either way. But now, supposing they do that and set out after us, then wouldn't it be a fine thing to jump into the ocean and soar off under their long skinny noses?"

She said with a sigh, "We'll compromise. We'll hide it so that it's accessible. But we'll go back to it only if we can't get a regular tourist packet to Badau. Assuming, of course, that we're successful here."

Paddy went to the chart of the planet. "That location is right on the lip of the cliff—North Cape, it's called, on Kolkhorit Island."

She said doubtfully, "I think your interpolations are slack. I got a point just off the cliff."

Paddy laughed. "Won't that be just like a woman? Her navigation sets us out in the ocean. You'll see that I'm right," he promised her. "We'll find what we're looking for on the edge of the cliff."

She shook her head. "The point's off the edge of the cliff." She glanced at him sidewise with raised eyebrows. "What's the matter?"

"You're too authoritative to suit the blood of one of the Skibbereen Blackthorns. We're a proud clan."

She smiled. "They'll never hear about it unless you tell them. And I'm only giving orders because I'm more efficient and smarter than you are."

"*Hah!*" cried Paddy. "Now then, you're as vain as the

Shaul jailer that did the cube roots in his head, and an arrogant cur he was, and he's still nursing the bruise I gave him. I'll do the same for you, my black-headed minx, if you're not less bothersome with your orders."

She made a mock obeisance. "Lead on, Sultan. Take it from here. You're the boss. Let's see how you handle it."

"Well," Paddy rubbed his chin, "at least we'll talk things over a bit and there won't be these lordly decisions. Here's my idea—we'll drop low over that gas ocean and make for the shore. We'll find a bit of quiet beach near the cliff, we'll drop down, seal our ship, get out and see what's to be done."

"Good enough," said Fay. "Let's go."

The gas ocean showed a queer roiling surface like slow-boiling water. In color it was the dirty yellow of oily smoke and the yellow light of Alpheratz penetrated only a few feet into the depths. From time to time the wind would scoop up a tall yellow tongue, lift it high, blow it over backwards.

Paddy brought the boat down almost to the surface, steered cautiously toward the lavender-blue bulk of Kolkhorit Island. The finger of the North Cape suddenly appeared through the haze with the sharp-cut silhouette of the cliff at the tip.

Paddy changed course and the cape loomed swiftly over them—a rocky tumble of porphyry, pegmatite, granite. He cut the power, the boat drifted close to shore. Below them appeared a small table, rimmed by walls of shadowed gray rock and almost awash in the seethe of brown gas. Paddy dropped the boat into the most secluded corner and five minutes later they stood on the barren windy rock with the ship sealed.

Paddy walked to the edge of the table, peered into the fog below. "Strange stuff." He turned. "Let's go."

They climbed up over the rocks and after a hundred yards scrambling across loose gravel, came out on a well-paved path. Fay clutched Paddy's sleeve.

"A couple of Eagles—there in the rocks. I hope they didn't see us land."

The Eagles hopped solemnly up to the path, man-creatures seven feet tall with leathery hide stretched tight over sharp bones, narrow skulls with jutting noses, little red eyes, foot-long crests of orange hair. They bore pouches bulging with red gelatinous globes like jellyfish.

Paddy watched them advancing with truculent eyes. "A more curious race was never bred. They'll want to know all about us. Ah, these planets are like cuckoo's eggs in a wren's nest and to think that Earth once spent her best on them."

He nodded to the Eagles. "Good morning, friend Eagles," he said in a syrupy voice. "And how's your bulb-picking today?"

"Good enough." They looked around the horizon. "Where's the little air-boat?"

"Air-boat? Ah, yes. It flew very swiftly to the east and out of sight in a twinkling."

The Eagles examined Paddy and Fay with sharp interest. "And what are you doing here along the shore?"

"Well now—" began Paddy. Fay interrupted him. "We're tourists walking up to the top of the North Cape. Could you tell us the best way?"

The Eagle motioned. "Just follow the path. It will lead into the Sunset Road. You're Earthers?" He spat slyly to the side.

"That we are—and as good as the best of you."

"Better," said Fay softly.

"What's your business on Alpheratz A?"

"Och, but we're fond of your lovely landscape, your marvelous cities. There's never sights like these on old Earth. Truth to tell, we're tourists, out to see the wonders of the universe."

The Eagles made a noise like "*Rrrrrr.*" Without further words they both set off down the path, muttering to each other.

Paddy and Fay, watching covertly, saw them pause, gesture along the horizon, point toward the rocks. But finally they continued along the path.

Fay said, "They were only a hundred yards from where you insisted on leaving the boat. It's just blind luck they didn't climb the rocks."

Paddy threw up his arms. "Like all women she will never miss the opportunity to crow at honest error. Lucky the day when I last see her skinny posterior walking away."

Fay's eyebrows rose. "Skinny? It's not either."

"Humph," said Paddy. "You don't get hams from a chicken."

"For my size it's just right," said Fay. "I've even had it pinched—once or twice."

Paddy made a face. "Faith, it's a sordid life you female agents live."

She cocked her head. "Perhaps not so sordid as you might think. And if you've finished deriding my figure and slandering my morals, we'll be off."

Paddy shook his head wonderingly, had no more to say. They turned their backs to the ocean of turbid gas, climbed the path the two Eagles had pointed out.

They gained a rocky meadow, passed a small village. Here they saw a central obelisk topped by a whirling-bladed fetish, concentric circles of conical houses, a long raised platform for the Pherasic pavanne-like dancing. A dozen Eagles, standing in a solemn group near a half-unpacked crate of machinery, looked like odd hybrids of man and stick-insect.

Fay said dreamily as they walked, "Isn't it a marvel, Paddy? When man first landed here he was man. In two generations the tall skinny ones predominated, in four the skull formation had begun. And now look at them. And to think that in spite of their appearance they're men. They can breed with true men and the same goes for the Asmasians, the Canopes, the Shauls—"

"Don't forget the Maevites!" cried Paddy enthusiastically. "Ah, them beautiful women!"

"—then there are the Loristanese, the Creepers, the Green-bags—and all the rest of the inbred overmen. It's truly wonderful how the planetary influence acts."

Paddy snorted. "Earth populates them and a hundred years later they come returning like curses to spite their grandsires."

Fay laughed. "We shouldn't be too arrogant, Paddy. It was the same differentiation and specialization that split the original simian stock into gorillas, chimpanzees, orangutans, a dozen types of submen—finally the true Cro-Magnon.

"The situation has backfired now, Paddy. Today we're the root stock, and all these splits and changes brought about by the differences in light, food atmosphere, gravity—they *may* produce a race as much better than men as men were superior to the protosimians."

Paddy snorted, "That I'll believe when—"

"Consider," said Fay seriously. "The Shauls can do complex mathematical operations in their heads. In a contest for survival that depended on mathematical ability they'd win. The Loristanese are psychically keen. They can telepathize to some extent, and they're subtle in person-to-person dealings. They're the merchants of the universe and wonders at group enterprise.

"These Eagles here—their curiosity is insatiable and they're so naturally persistent that there's no word for the quality in their language. Any more than the Earthers have a word for the will to live.

"Men will shrug off a problem or a task but the Eagles will work till they've accomplished what they've started. The Asmasians have that pineal pleasure lobe. It doesn't give them much survival value but how they enjoy their lives! Sometimes I wish I were an Asmasian."

Paddy said contemptuously, "I've heard all of that in grade school. The Kotons are the ruthless chess players, the daring ones, the soldiers. I think of them as the devils that figured out the most horrible tortures. Then there's the Canopes, that hive together like bees. What of it? None of them have a little of everything like the Earthers."

Fay said seriously, "That's by our standards. We're taking ourselves as the base of comparison. By the standards of these other races we're at one extreme or another."

Paddy grumbled, "Better that old Sam Langtry had smothered in his cradle. Look at the mess and jumble, men of all varieties. It was so simple before."

Fay tilted her head back, laughed. "Don't be silly, Paddy. Human history has always been a series—a cycle of differentiation, then the mingling of the surviving stock back to uniformity. Right now we're going through the cycle of differentiation."

"And may the best man win," said Paddy dourly.

"So far," said Fay, "we're not winning."

Paddy shoved out his head, crooked his elbows.

"Well, they went and tied up the space-drive on us. That's like blindfolding a man before he gets in a free-for-all. Give us Earthers an even crack at it—we'd have 'em backed to the boards, crying and pleading for mercy. What a joke! It was an Earther that discovered the gadget and gave them their lives."

"Accident," said Fay, kicking at a pebble. "Langtry was only trying to accelerate mesons in a tungsten cylinder."

"That's the man who's responsible for all this trouble!" cried Paddy. "Langtry! If I had the spalpeen here I'd give him a piece of my mind."

"I would too," said Fay. "But mostly for giving the secret to his five sons instead of the Earth Parliament."

"Well—the five sons, then. Greedy devils, they're the ones I'd rail at. What did they need, each with a planet to himself?"

Fay made a careless gesture. "Love of power. The empire-building instinct. Or bad blood. Call it anything you like. They left Earth for the stars and settled along the Langtry line, each to a world, and set themselves up in the business of selling space-drives to the home world. Their descendants get the secret, no one else. I suppose nobody would be more surprised than old Sam Langtry at the way things have turned out."

"If I had him here, you know what I'd be doing with him?"

"Yes—you told me. You'd be giving him a piece of your mind."

"Ah, you're mocking me now. But no, I'd send him back to guard our boat. And we'd beat his bones raw if divil an Eagle laid a finger on the polish."

Fay looked up the ridge ahead. "You'd better be saving your breath for the climbing."

VI

The road bent up toward North Peak in a gradually steepening rise. Below and to their right spread the sea of dull gas, out as far as the eye could reach. Back along the shore the whirling fetishes of a thousand little villages flashed in the yellow light of Alpheratz. To the left, around the hook of the cape, was Sugksu, a city built on the same general plan as the villages. There was a central obelisk, surrounding circles of buildings.

Fay clutched Paddy's arm. "Look! See there— maybe you're right after all...."

It was a spindly trestle of steel, crowned with a whirling fetish, on the very lips of the cliff.

"Those things are sacred to something or somebody. We'll have to look for a Sacred Sign."

Standing around the edge of the cliff was a group of Eagles, males with scarlet or orange-dyed crests, females with greens and blues, all wearing the same black-brown sheath of fabric that covered their bony bodies from breast to knee, the same flat shoes.

"Tourists," whispered Fay. "We'll have to wait till they leave."

"Naturally," said Paddy.

For twenty minutes they waited, looking out over the vast spread of view, eyeing the Eagles sidelong.

A voice spoke at their elbow. An eagle had stepped up beside them unnoticed. Paddy's Adam's apple twitched. The Eagle wore the official medallion of the Pherasic government.

"Tourists?" asked the Eagle.

"We're loving every minute of it," said Fay enthusiastically. "The view is marvelous! The city is beautiful...."

The Eagle nodded. "It is indeed. This is one of our finest spectacles. Even the Revered Son of Langtry himself ascends from time to time to take the north airs."

Fay glanced at Paddy significantly. Paddy raised one eyebrow. Evidently the death of the five Sons had not been announced to the universe at large. The Eagle was saying, "And when you get down to Sugksu be sure to take the deep-sea tour and see the strange sights under the gas. Have you been on the planet long?"

"Not too long. But we've lost track of time," she added coyly. "You see, we're on our honeymoon. But we couldn't resist coming to see Alpheratz A."

The Eagle nodded sagely. "Wise—very wise. We have a world from which much may be learned." And he stalked on.

Paddy spat. "Damned meddlers. It's hard to know when their curiosity is official and when it's just curiosity."

"Sh," said Fay. "They're leaving."

Three minutes later the top of the peak was bare to the sweep of the wind.

"Now," said Fay. "A Sacred Sign—where is it? And how do you know it's sacred when we see it?"

Paddy vaulted up on the base of the trestle, glanced appraisingly up at the spinning vanes of orange and blue and red. "That whirlymagig must be it."

He scrambled up like a monkey until he came under the sweeping blades. He reached up, wrenched down the whole tangle of fiber, metal and feathers.

Fay yelled, "You fool! They can see that from below!"

Paddy said, "I had to if I wanted to see what was under."

"Well—what *is* under?"

"Nothing," Paddy said uncomfortably.

"Get down then for heaven's sake. The riot squad will be here in five minutes."

They walked briskly down the slope. Hardly had they gone a hundred yards when Fay put out her hand. "Listen!"

A fierce anxious sound, still faint—*Sweeee—eeeeee—eeeee*. Far below a pair of motorcycles turned into the road, started up the grade. The sound grew louder, keening, whining. It stopped short. A moment later two Eagles, each with the official medallion on his uniform, roared to a halt beside them.

One alighted. "Who caused the destruction? He who is guilty will receive the severest of treatments."

Fay said in a worried voice "We're not guilty. It was a party of Kotons and they went down the other way, I think."

"There *is* no other way."

"Ah, but they were wearing sky skates," said Paddy hopefully.

"They were drunk, the scoundrels," said Fay.

The Eagle officials inspected them skeptically. Paddy sighed, cracked his knuckles behind his back. He speculated about the Pherasic jails. Were they more comfortable, he wondered, than the old brick fort at Akhabats?

The chief of the Eagles said to the subordinate, "I'll continue to the top. You wait here. We will presume them guilty until I find otherwise."

He twisted power on his motorcycle, continued up the hill.

"We're in the soup, Paddy," said Fay in Earth-talk. "I'll distract his attention. We want that motorbike."

Paddy stared at her, aghast. "It's a long chance."

"Of course it is," she snapped. "It's our *only* chance. We've got to get away. If they arrest us, march us in, check our psychographs..."

Paddy grimaced. "Very well."

Fay stepped around in front of the wheel. The Eagle blew his cheeks out, pulled back his narrow head.

"Clout him, Paddy," yelled Fay.

The Eagle turned his head just in time to meet Paddy's fist. In a great thrash of rickety arms and legs the Eagle sprawled over backwards into the road.

"Now we've really done it," said Paddy ruefully. "It's long years picking oakum for this."

"Shut up—jump on that bike. Let's get moving," panted Fay.

"I don't know how to run the thing," Paddy grumbled.

"*Run* it! We'll coast! Let's go!"

Paddy threw his leg over the narrow seat and Fay jumped on behind. He turned it downhill, threw levers till he found the brake. With a lurch the motorcycle started.

"Whee!" yelled Fay in Paddy's ear. "This is like the roller coaster at Santa Cruz."

Paddy stared big-eyed down the hill and the wind whipped water from his eyes.

"I don't know how to stop her!" yelled Paddy. "I can't remember where the brake is!" The rush of wind tore the words from his lips. He pulled frantically at unfamiliar knobs, levers, handles and at last chanced on a pedal that seemed to have some effect.

"Watch that side road," screamed Fay in his ear. "It goes down to the city!"

Paddy leaned and the motorcycle screeched around a party of pedestrians, who shouted raucous insults at their backs. And now to Paddy's horror the brake pedal had lost its effect.

"Slow down, Paddy," cried Fay. "For heaven's sake, you reckless fool—"

"I wish I could," grinned Paddy. "It's my dearest wish."

"Throw in the drive!" She leaned past him, pointed. "There—try that knob!"

Paddy pulled the lever a notch toward him. There was a loud whine and the motorcycle slowed so rapidly as almost to toss them off. It wobbled to a halt. Paddy put out his leg.

"Get off," hissed Fay. "There's that little path, and right over that ridge of rock is our boat."

Sweeee=eeeee-eeee-eeee! From far above them a nerve-tingling sound, urgent and shrill.

"Here comes the other," said Paddy. "Swooping like a panther."

"Run," said Fay. "Over the ridge. We've got to get to our ship and fast."

SWEEE-EEEEE-EEEEE!

"Too late," said Paddy. "He'd shoot us while we ran. Come here with me. Watch this now."

He pulled her off the road, down behind a rock.

The sound of the motor increased in volume but dropped in pitch as the officer approached slowly, cautiously. He trundled past the boulder.

"*Boo!*" yelled Paddy, jumping out. The Eagle squawked. Paddy heaved at the handlebars, the motorcycle left the path, bounded, bumped down a steep ravine. The last they saw was the Eagle frantically trying to steer the machine around outcrops and boulders, his crest tense, elbows wide, legs spraddled out into the air.

There was a crash, then silence.

Paddy sighed. Fay said, "You're not so smart. You wouldn't believe me when I said the point was not on the cliff but at the base."

Paddy was disposed to argue. "How could it be? There was the Sacred Sign just as the sheet said."

"Nonsense," said Fay. "You'll see."

Their boat had not been touched. They crawled in, sealed the port, Fay climbed into the pilot's seat. "You keep watch."

She lifted the boat, slid it off the table, let it sink under the gas, which showed luminous yellow through the observation window.

"The color is from suspended dust," said Fay off-handedly. "The gas is dense and the dust seeks the level of its own specific gravity and there it floats forever. A little deeper the gas will be clear—or so I've been told."

"What's the composition of the gas?" asked Paddy. "Or is it known?"

"It's neon kryptonite."

"That's a strange pairing," remarked Paddy.

"It's a strange gas," replied Fay tartly.

Now she let the boat fall. The sun-drenched dust disappeared and they found themselves looking out at a marvelous new landscape. It was like nothing else either had seen before, like nothing imagined.

The yellow light of Alpheratz was toned to an old gold suffusion, a tawny light that changed the landscape below to an unreal hazy fairyland. Underneath them was a great valley with hills and dales fading off into golden murk. To the left loomed the great cliff of Kolkhorit Island, rising up and out of sight above. Fay followed the cliff till it jutted out, fell back.

"There's North Cape," she said. "And there on the little plateau—that's exactly the right spot."

Paddy said in a subdued voice, "Yes, by all that's holy, you seem to be right for once."

"Look," said Fay. "See that thing like a sundial? That's what we want."

Paddy said dubiously, "How're we to get it?"

She said angrily, "In your spacesuit, of course! And hurry! They'll be after us any minute."

Paddy gloomily let himself out through the space lock, stalked across the plateau. Bathed in the eerie golden light he advanced on the pedestal. On its face was inlaid a red and gold pentagram.

He tried to lift—nothing happened. He pushed, felt a quiver, a wrench. He put his shoulder down, heaved. The pedestal fell over. In a little lead-lined cavity was a brass cylinder.

Badau lay below, an opulent blue-green planet with a thick blanket of atmosphere.

Paddy pinched Fay's calves, felt her thighs. She jerked, turned to him a startled glance.

"Now, now—I was merely testing to see if you might be fit to walk on the planet," explained Paddy. "You'll be monstrous heavy, you know."

Fay laughed ruefully. "I thought for a moment you were making love Skibbereen-style."

Paddy screwed up his features. "You're not my type. It's the cow-girls of Maeve for me. Now—as I've just discovered—you've hardly enough flesh to keep the air away from your bones. You're so pale and peaked. No, for some you might do but not for Paddy Blackthorn."

But he was smiling and she laughed back and Paddy said, "In truth, sometimes when you've got that devil's gleam in your eye you're showing your teeth in a grin, you're almost pretty in a puckish sort of way."

"Thank you very much. Enough of the blarney. Where are we going?"

"It's a place called the Kamborogian Arrowhead."

"And where's that, I wonder?"

Paddy studied the charts. "There's no mention of it here. It sounds like an inn or hotel or something of the sort. Once we land we'll be able to find out for sure. And you'll be frightful tired, for the gravity's strong as a bull here."

"I'm not worried about the gravity," said Fay. "I'm worried whether or not the Badau police have received our description yet."

Paddy pursed his lips. "Badau's a popular place with Earth tourists, gravity or none. Though why they come surpasses my understanding, since it's nothing but insults and slights and arrogance they get from the Hunks, the conceited omadhauns."

"It's a very beautiful planet," mused Fay. "So gentle and green-looking with those million little lakes and rolling valleys."

"There're no mountains," said Paddy, "because the water tears them down as fast as they're pushed up."

"What do you call that?" Fay pointed to a tremendous palisade flung across the countryside.

"Ah, that's a big segment of land being pulled *down*," said Paddy. "With so much gravity there's these great movements of the crust and these great cliffs. The Badaus build dams across all the waterfalls and make use of the power. Then the water doesn't tear a great gully into the land."

"Land, land, land," said Fay. "That first Son of Langtry was a glutton for land."

"And the Langtry clan still owns all Badau. It's a feudalism or so it says in the book. Langtrys own the big estates, rent out to lesser noblemen, who rent out again, and sometimes there's another subletting and another until it's the little farmer that's supporting them all.

"And marvelous crops they grow here, Fay. The finest fruits and vegetables—all Earth imports, since the original growth was rank poison. And the plants have changed as much as the men when they came to be Badaus."

Paddy looked at Fay earnestly. "This is Mary's own truth now I'm telling you and as I'm Patrick Delorcy Blackthorn I've been here before and I know the country. You won't believe it when you see oranges growing on vines and them as big as pumpkins.

"And they grow a wheat that comes in heads the size of my foot, low to the ground, with a pair of leaves like lilypads. They've got grapes now with a brittle end that you knock off and a gallon of wine pours out. They're marvelous good botanists, these Badaus."

Fay was studying the chart. "There's Slettevold—that's the largest city. A clearing house for export and import, it says. We could land there and maybe have our boat vapor-plated. A nice dull green instead of this gunmetal. I don't think we'd be conspicuous."

Paddy squinted down at the wide bright face of Badau. "There's such a lather of little boats flipping in and out of here that an Earther would hardly believe it, not knowing the secrets of Langtry's sons. One little space-boat the more or the less will hardly be looked at."

"They might think it strange for Earthers to own a space-boat. Not many do. Mostly they come by the passenger packets."

Paddy rubbed his chin. "If we land at Outer Slett Field about dusk—there's no control or examination there—we should be able to walk into Slettevold without question."

"It's about dusk now at Slettevold," said Fay. "There's the field so let's set down before they send a warhead up after us."

Outer Slett Field lay behind the warehouses and packing sheds which lined the main field. It was a wide irregular space, undeveloped, used by private owners, small traders. There was no control tower, no radar beam, and when Paddy and Fay climbed out into the warm dusk no eye turned to look after them.

Paddy took a few steps, turned to watch Fay walking toward him—slowly as if she were wearing a heavy knapsack. He grinned.

"Bed will be the finest thing you ever felt, young lady. Your knees will be like oiled hinges and your feet will ache as if they'd been trod by a horse. But in a day or so you'll not notice so much. And if you stayed here a while your neck would swell and your sons would grow up short and tough and rubbery and your grandsons would be Hunks as coarse and ugly as the best of 'em."

Fay sniffed. "Not if I have the picking, as I intend, of their father." She stared around the luminous blue-green sky. "Where's the town from here, Mr. Baedeker?"

Paddy gestured toward a grove of low heavy-trunked trees at the edge of the field. "If memory serves me there's a tube-station in this direction. It'll take us to the heart of the town."

Painfully they walked to the concrete ramp which led down to a pair of metal doors. Paddy pressed twice. A moment later the doors snapped back and they entered a little car with two seats.

The doors slid shut, there was a sense of rapid motion. A moment later the doors opened to the sounds of the city.

Fay looked at Paddy "Free? Doesn't someone make us pay?"

Paddy said, "All the utilities were put in by the Langtry family. They're so wealthy that they don't need our miserly coins. *Noblesse oblige.* We're on the biggest family estate in the universe."

They stepped out on a broad street lined with low heavy buildings, all with plate-glass fronts on the lower levels. Fay read a legend on the portico of a long arcade. "'Skettevold Inn'—that sounds good. Let's get ourselves a bath and some fresh food."

"*Hah!*" Paddy laughed. "That's not for the likes of us, young lady. We're Earthers. They'd not let us past the doors."

Fay stared incredulously. "Do you mean that they wouldn't serve us merely because we're—"

Paddy nodded. "That's right. The Earther keeps his place on Badau."

Fay turned away. "I'm too tired to argue. Let's go to the Earther hotel."

VII

The Kamborogian Arrowhead? The desk clerk, a sour-visaged Badau, told them it was a resort on the shores of the Iath Lake. To Fay's diffident inquiry he smirked wryly.

"Earthers at the Kamborogian? They'd as soon serve a run of lard-legs. You must understand the quality of Badau take their pleasure at the Kamborogian. It's where the Son himself goes. Everything must be quiet and elegant."

Paddy nodded. "Ah—then we miserable Earthers would be out of place indeed."

Fay asked desperately, "Don't Earthers go there at all?"

"Only as scullions or entertainers. The Ryeville Ramblers, a trio of acrobats, just returned from an engagement and were well satisfied with their treatment."

"Hmm." Paddy rubbed his chin. "How does one get these engagements?"

The clerk turned away. "Oh—through the amusement syndic, I suppose."

Paddy turned to Fay. "Now, young lady, can you dance, sing, mimic, eat fire, or turn handsprings?"

Fay said, "I'm no acrobat, not in this gravity. I suppose I could play a comb or recite Gunga Din with gestures."

"I'm a magician," said Paddy. "I perform card tricks that'll mystify them, especially if they're drunk as they're apt to be. We'll be the finest act ever brought on the floor. At least we'll be allowed on the premises."

The Kamborogian Arrowhead was a block of concrete five stories high and a quarter mile long, ornamented with a profusion of gold quincunxes, quatrefoils, fleurs-de-lis. Alternate sections were stained pink and light green and the overhanging pediment was light blue.

Iath Lake, rippling, twinkling very swiftly to the strong gravity, half encircled the building and the formal gardens. Beyond, the land fell away in a vast sweep of rolling turf up to a mile-high cliff, running horizon to horizon.

The air of wealth and opulence clung to the hotel. It glistened with crystal panes and bright metal. The canopies glowed like satin. Oval shell-like pleasure boats rode the lake, moving under small square sails.

Paddy and Fay discreetly went to the rear, entered a waiting room, stated their business to a tired-looking Asmasian porter, who brought them to the Chief Steward in a brightly lit office.

The Chief Steward was short and fat even for a Badau. His jowls hung like the wattles on a chicken. His eyes were deep-set and clever.

Paddy said, "The gentleman at the Amusement Syndicate sent us up here to see you. We're Black and Black, Entertainers Extraordinary."

The steward looked them up, down, ran his eyes

over Fay's figure. Like some of the other planetary races the Badaus found Earther women attractive. "Did not the Syndic give you a card for me?"

"Ah, we lost it," said Paddy. "The wind blew it clean out of my hands and away in a twinkling. However the Syndic was much pleased with us and said to say a kind word to you for him."

"What do you do?"

"I'm a magician," said Paddy. "I'm an accomplished prestidigitator and objects come and go at my command. I change water into purple vapor and then to a swarm of frogs and they melt into a big flash of light. But my specialty is with the cards. I make the ace of spades jump out of the deck and bow from the waist, and there's a trick I know with the kings and queens that'll have 'em giggling for months to come.

"Then there's my wife here. She's the cleverest thing alive. She's great. She'll have them agog with their eyes so you could knock them off with sticks. Sure, they'll clap your back for giving them such rare enjoyment."

The steward blinked. "Well—the listing is complete. I'll give you a try and if you're as good as you say I'll let another team go that's not doing so well."

"Good," said Paddy. "A chance is all we want. We'll be sleeping in the hotel tonight then?"

"Yes, this way. I'll show you to the entertainers' barracks. I'll have to separate you."

"Ah, no!" cried Paddy.

"Sorry—it's the rules of the establishment."

Paddy found himself in a long hall, lined with tubs full of sleep-foam and small closets opposite. The steward assigned him a section and said, "You will be fed with a chow cart in half an hour. When it's time for your act, about the fourteenth phase, you will be summoned.

"Until then, you can rest or rehearse as you wish. The practice room is through that door. There is to be no loud talking, no quarrelling, no alcohol or narcotics. Under no circumstances are Earthers permitted to wander on the grounds."

"Faith," muttered Paddy, "I hope you'll let me use the bathroom."

"What's that? What's that?"

"I was inquiring about my wife," said Paddy smoothly. "When do I see her?"

"The recreation hall is open tomorrow. Until then she'll be well enough." He departed, a little ball of hard brown flesh in an embroidered surcoat.

Paddy looked up and down the barracks. A few of the sleeping tubs held the bodies of low-caste Shauls, Asmasians, Canopes, the long-limbed Hepetanthroids of New Hellas, a few other Earthers.

In the tub next to him lay a Labirite from Deneb Ten, a small mottled anthropoid with arms like lengths of cable and flabby hands. He was watching Paddy with blind-looking eyes.

"What's your act, Earther?" he asked in the Badaic language.

"I'm a magician," replied Paddy morosely.

"A good one, it is to be presumed?"

"The best. Flames—lore of the little folk..." Paddy's voice died to a mutter.

"You'd better be good," said the Labirite. "A night or so ago they saw through a magician's tricks and they threw food at him."

Paddy raised his eyebrows. "Are they then so finicky, these Hunks?"

The Labirite said, "Indeed they are. Never forget,

here is the cream of Badau, only the Langtry clan and maybe one or two of the highest lords otherwise. There's a convention on now and they're more than usually excitable, vehement, abrupt. And if they chose to stick you with one of their poniards no one would think twice about it."

"Whisht, whisht!" muttered Paddy. "And me with my cat's cradle tricks." Aloud he said, "And where might Suite 10 be?"

The Labirite turned his prunelike eyes away. "I don't know. One of the porters will tell you. If it's stealing you plan don't get caught."

"Indeed, no stealing," said Paddy. "In Suite 10 is an old friend I'm looking for."

The Labirite stared. "One of the Badau Langtrys friend to an Eather? Well, I suppose stranger things have happened. Did you save his life?"

Paddy made an absentminded answer, lay back thinking. Any entrance to Suite 10 must be made very soon, because after one performance there would be no further opportunity. He pictured himself dodging food scraps, ejected from the hotel with curses and insults.

He rose to his feet, set off down the hall. He turned into a corridor with stone walls like a dungeon, lit by a light tube along the top. He came to an open archway, looked through saw a counter, a wicket, stores of material and behind them a Canope clerk.

Paddy advanced with a swagger and said, "I'm the new porter. The Chief Steward told me to get my outfit here."

The Canope clerk wheezed, rose to his feet, reached into a bin, tossed a white bumper on the counter, opened a drawer, pulled out white gloves and a masklike inhaler. "They don't like the air we breath,

Earther. Wear the mask over your mouth and nose at all times. Here's your cap, your sandals, your cleaning kit. Good luck and step lively."

"Indeed I will and I'm forever grateful to you. Where may Suite 10 be found?"

"Suite 10? The steward assigns you to Suite 10 on your first day? Strange. That's the Son's private library and very hoity-toity too. Go out the door there, turn to the right along the corridor with the rose quartz floor and so on till you come to a statue of the Badau Langtry.

"If there's anyone within do not enter, because they're mighty secret and irascible at this time and they don't like Earthers. For some reason they're merciless to the Earthers."

I could tell you why, thought Paddy. He hastily donned the porter's garments, set off down the corridor.

A narrow door took him from dingy stone into a world of exquisite delicacy and sparkle. The Badaus were clever craftsmen with a love of intricate design and the great hall was walled with a mosaic of rare minerals—jade, lapis, sparkling yellow wulfenite, red chert, jasper, carnelian. The floor was slabbed with bands of rose quartz and an oily black obsidian.

He passed a line of arches opening into a high lobby swimming in a greenish-yellow light. Sitting among clumps of vegetation were groups of the Badaus, conversing, sipping wine or inhaling stimulating confections from tubes.

Paddy moved along with as little ostentation as possible and the gravity helped provide him with a servile crouch. Ahead he saw a statue, a Badau in an heroic posture.

"Ha," said Paddy angrily, "they don't even admit any more that Sam Langtry was an Earther. Now look at Sam Langtry's own son, as true an Earther as Paddy Blackthorn himself, and look how they show him, a scrunched-up wart of a Badau."

Beside the statue was a high door or carved rosewood. Paddy glanced quickly up and down the hall— no one was close. He put his ear to the door—no sound. He stretched out his hand to the latch button. Behind came a scrape and the door snapped back. Paddy bowed, sidled to one side, stooped, pretended to be picking up a spot of dust.

The Badau stepped out, paused, turned a long glance down at Paddy. Another followed him out of the room.

"Spies, spies everywhere," said the first in a bitter voice. "A man can hardly go for a sail on the lake without some Earther pushing his head up from the water." He turned away. Paddy sighed, watched the broad muscular back with a limp feeling in his knees.

The Badau's voice came back to him. "They're like rodents. Everywhere. Indefatigable. To think that one of them...If there were only means to apprehend—" His voice became an indistinct mutter.

Paddy grimaced, eased the muscles at the corner of his mouth, pushed open the door. The first chamber of Suite 10 was empty. It was a large library, with shelves of books running up the walls. A great oval table occupied the center of the room and at the end stood a small screen and file for microfilm. An arch opened into chambers beyond but here was his destination.

He glanced around the walls. Books, books, books—thousand of them, with a subtle air of disuse. He could not inspect each one separately. Where was the catalog? There, a small case beside the microfilm viewer. He pulled it open, fumbled through his mind for the Badaic alphabet.

The Foolish Man's Inclination. There it was, Block Five, Shelf Twelve.

Paddy looked along the shelves, found Block Five in a far corner. Shelf Twelve was at the top.

How to get up? He spied a ladder running on a bronze track across the room, and pushed it around to Block Five. He climbed up to Shelf Twelve, ran his eye down the titles.

The Complete Philosophy of Kobame Biankul...Archaeological Studies at Zabmir...Relation of Planetary Environment to Housing Modes...A Scientist Looks at Aquilan Disk-worms...Neophasm...Botanical Dictionary...The Foolish Man's Inclination.

Paddy drew it from its place, tucked it in the pouch which held his cleaning equipment. A voice from below said, "Porter. Come down here."

The words were like chisels. Paddy nearly fell from the ladder, bumped his head on the shelf as he looked down. The same two Badaus that had surprised him at the door stood looking up. He noticed on the chest of the foremost the medallion of a Councillor to the Son.

"Porter. Come down here."

Paddy descended the ladder. "Yes indeed, your lordship."

The small yellow eyes bored into his. "What were you doing up there?"

"Dusting the books, your lordship."

"There's no dust here. These books are sacred, forbidden to your touch."

"Well, I thought I'd better make sure. I didn't want your lordships sneezing for my neglect."

"What book did you take from the shelf?"

"Book, sir?"

"Give it to me."

Paddy twitched, leaned forward, leaned back. Two Badaus—short but burly, hardened to the gravity of the planet, while he was under the strain of the added weight. They could handle him as easily as he might best a six-year-old child.

"Oh, the book! Well, your lordships, it was just a bit of reading for my spare time. Thanking you for your attention, but I'd better be about my duties or the steward will be calling me to account."

Paddy started to sidle away. Two arms seized him, the book was taken from his pouch.

The Badau glanced at the title. *"The Foolish Man's Inclination*—well-selected, I must say. Hmm." He looked back at Paddy. "Strange interests for a porter. And you can read Badaic?"

"It was a whim of the moment, sir, and I but meant to look at the pictures."

The second Badau said, "Better call Intelligence, have them put the man through investigation."

The Councillor hesitated. "They're occupied with that off-planet business, all working for the reward." He grunted. "Now it's a million marks a year for life, amnesty for all crimes past and future. If it gets much better I'll be out looking for the fellow myself."

He released Paddy. "I suppose an Earther stealing a book is no world-shaking event."

The Councillor shoved Paddy roughly toward the door. "See that you mind your duties."

Paddy said, "Please may I have the book, your lordship?"

The Badau's face became rigid with sudden rage, Paddy ran off as nimbly as the gravity would permit. As he left the room he caught a glimpse of the Badau glancing at the book curiously.

In the fury, fear, frustration, Paddy returned to the servants' quarter. He doffed the porter's garb, found his way to the barracks. The Chief Steward was standing by his sleep-tub.

"So *there* you are! This way, hurry! There's been an opening and I'll put you on now. Get your equipment."

"Just a deck of cards," said Paddy wearily. How would he tell Fay? She, who depended on his resource and cleverness... They must leave. If the Councillor came to page 100 he'd call for the Chief Steward and inquire about the strangely literate porter.

Paddy said to the Steward, "I think I'd better see my wife a moment."

"Get *in* there!" screeched the Steward. "Before I cudgel you! You'll see your wife at the proper time."

The exit was barred. Paddy dispiritedly followed the steward. Any minute now the furor would ring out. Ah well, shrugged Paddy, death came to all men. Perhaps the Councillor had merely replaced the book.

More hopefully he followed the Steward up a ramp into an antechamber off the performance platform. The Steward turned him over to a Badau in a red and green tunic. "Here he is—the magician. I've had to search the entire building for him."

The Badau in uniform inspected Paddy sharply. "Where's your equipment?"

"Just let me have a deck of cards," said Paddy. "That's all I need for now."

"On that shelf then. Now attend carefully. You're on after the present act. Step up on the stage, bow to the diners. See that your humor, if you make use of such, is of a refined nature, the Lords are at their eating. Bow when you leave the stage. Conduct yourself with the utmost respect. This is not some greasy tavern on Earth."

Paddy nodded, went to stand by the entrance to the stage, where an Earther woman was performing an exotic dance. Music came from a band of mesh around the stage, the music of a climate as warm and enchanting as the dance.

The Badau audience was attentive, watchful. Damned satyrs, thought Paddy, and turned his own attention to the dance, a writhing, posturing slow gyration. The girl wore a gilded G-string over hips slender but ripe, a shoulder blouse of gauze, a high pagodalike headdress. She was sinuous as running water. Here movements were pulse-stirring promises of joy.

The music waxed, waned, became melodious, piquant, soft, increased in beat toward a climax. The dancer followed like shadows after a cloud. Twine of arms, heave of smooth lithe torso, twist of round legs, collapse in a curtsy and off the stage.

"*Phew!*" said Paddy, eyes glittering. "There'd be a good shipmate for me and I'd even forget the Maeve women."

"The Magician Black unveils the ancient arcana and the mysteries of Earth," said a voice to the audience.

"Go on," said the stage manager. "Perform. Make it good."

Paddy halted, backed up like a skittish horse. The time had come. This was reality. There was a room full of Badau lords to be entertained. They were dull, unsympathetic, hostile. Of course he could jolly them a bit, get them in a good humor.

The stage manager jostled him forward. "Go on, get out there," he said, "and don't forget my instructions."

Paddy felt naked on the stage. "Ladies and gentlemen, now you're to see marvels such as you've never suspected. So sit tight. I have here a deck of fifty-two cards—the oldest playing device known to man, other than the chessboard. And I'm proud to say there's none that's more a master of the pack than me, Harry Black, the Miracle Magician of the Age."

Behind his back he covertly split the deck. "Now I'll read you the cards in a way you'll talk about for years to come."

He held the cards before his face. "This first one doesn't count. I only want to show you the deck." Behind his back, out again. "Now this is the jack of spades—trey of clubs—five of diamonds—" The audience seemed apathetic. He heard a muffled hiss.

"Enough of that, you say? Very well then, 'twas only a warm-up. Now here's the jumping aces. Just a minute, I'll turn my back on you to count the cards. Now, see here, that the ace of clubs, the ace of spades and in the middle the ace of diamonds. You can tell by the point.

"Now see—I put one on top, one in the middle, one on the bottom. I cut the cards. That's mixing them thoroughly. Now we look through the deck and there! What do you see! They're all together again."

Ssss...ssss...!

"And now," said Paddy genially, "if some kind gentleman would come forward, take a card.... Please someone?...Someone to draw a card?...All a little bashful, eh?...Very well, then, I'll draw one myself but it's you that'll see it and not Harry Black.

"Ah, and this little item it is—can you all see it now?—and I put it on the bottom and now I'll cut the cards, thus burying the card inextricably in the deck. And now here we go. Harry Black, with his trained glance, looks along the faces and with his eyesight keen as the fox of the Wicklows he spots the card and whisht! It's the nine of hearts! And isn't that a marvel now?"

Paddy ducked. It was the rind of a fruit buzzing past his ears. Paddy bowed. "Thank you, ladies and gentlemen, that'll be all for now."

He backed off the stage. "Cold audience," he remarked to the silent stage manager. "Ah, where's my wife?"

The manager said in a crisp voice, "If it weren't for her I'd have your thrown out of the hotel."

Paddy said stupidly, "And how do you mean if it weren't for her?"

The stage manager said contemptuously, "You saw her dance. The Lords seemed to like her. I advise you to stay in your bed tonight."

A great light burnt into Paddy's brain. "Dance? You mean that she was...You mean..." He beat at his brows. "And that was...Ah well, never mind. Where is the little deceiver?"

"She's in the dressing room, waiting for the next series."

"I've got to see her." Paddy ran down the ramp, bumped into Fay coming around the corner.

"We've got to leave," whispered Paddy. "They'll be after us at any time."

"Why the rush?" asked Fay, coolly.

"I went to Suite 10 to get the book. I just had it in my grasp when the hardest-looking Councillor of them all walks in and takes it clean away from me. As soon as he sees what's in it and decides what it is he'll have the hounds out after us, all of them. The sooner we're off the better." Paddy paused for breath while Fay looked on with a slight smile.

Paddy heaved a great sigh, rumpled his black hair. "No, no—it's no good. You go off, wait for me in the ship. I'm going now to find that hulking big Badau and I'll take that book away from him. I'll get it, and no mistake.

"But you be off, so they won't catch both of us. Besides," and he looked narrowly toward the stage manager, "I don't think they're planning anything good for you this night."

"Paddy," said Fay, "we'll both go. And the Badau will find nothing in the book. I got there first and I got the Son's memorandum. It's in my shoe right now. The sooner we're back on our ship the better."

VIII

Paddy awoke from deep sleep to find the ship floating free. He peered out a bull's-eye. Space surrounded them like a vast pool of clear water. Astern glittered Scheat, to one side hung yellow Alpheratz, and ahead down a foreshortened line ran the stars of Andromeda's body—Adhil the train. Mirach the loins, Almach the shoulder.

Paddy unzipped the elastic sheet, clambered out, stepped into the shower, stripped, turned on the mist. The foam searched his pores, slushed out oil, dust, perspiration. A blast of warm air dried him.

He dressed, stepped up to the bridge deck, where he found Fay bending over the chart table, her dark hair tousled, the line of her profile as clean and delicate as a mathematical curve.

Paddy scowled. Fay was wearing her white blouse, dark green slacks and sandals and seemed very calm and matter-of-fact. To his mind's eye came the picture of the near-naked dancer in the fantastic gilt headdress. He saw the motion of her cream-colored body.

The clench of muscles, the abandoned tilt of her head. And this was the same girl.

Fay looked up into his eyes and, as if divining his thoughts, smiled faintly, maddeningly.

Paddy maintained an injured silence, as if somehow Fay had cheated him. Fay, for motives of her own, did nothing to soothe him but turned back to the sheet of metal she had taken from the Badau book. After a minute she leaned back, handed it to Paddy.

It was minutely engraved in the Badaic block. The first paragraph described the space-drive tube, giving optimum dimensions, composition, the tri-axial equations for its inner and outer surfaces.

The second paragraph specified the type of fieldcoils found to be most efficient. Then followed two columns of five-digit numbers, three to a column, which Paddy—remembering the secret room at Akhabats he had broken into—knew to be field-strength settings.

Fay said, "I opened the Pherasic can, looked into it also. It had a metal sheet something that one—describing the tube—but instead of detailing the coils it prescribed their spacing."

Paddy nodded. "Duplication of information."

"We've got two of these things," said Fay seriously, "and it's uncomfortable carrying them around with us."

"I've been thinking the same thing," said Paddy. "And since we can't get in to Earth— Well, let's see. Delta Frianguli is pretty handy and there's an uninhabited planet."

The planet was dead and dull as a clinker, showing a reticulated surface of black plains and random flows of cratered scoria three miles high, ten miles wide.

Paddy made an abrupt gesture. "The problem is not so much hiding our loot as finding it again ourselves."

"It's a big planet," said Fay dubiously. "One spot looks like another."

"It's a misfit among planets," declared Paddy. "A dirty outcast, shunned by police society—all ragged and grimy and patched. Sure, I'd hate to be afoot down there in the waste."

"There," said Fay. "*There's* a landmark—that pillar or volcanic neck or whatever it is."

They settled to the black sand of the plain and it creaked harshly under the ship. The pillar rose high above them.

"Look at the face it makes." Paddy pointed out fancied features in the rock.

"Like an angry dragon or a gorgon."

"Angry Dragon Peak—that's its name," said Paddy. "And now there must be a cubbyhole somewhere near."

In their spacesuits they crossed the level space, the black sand crunching and squeaking underfoot, climbed the tumble of rock, and found a fissure at the base of the monolith.

"Now," said Fay, "somehow we've got to locate Angry Dragon Peak on the planet. We could cruise months around these badlands looking for it."

"Here's how we'll find it," said Paddy. "We'll take a head bubble from one of the spare spacesuits, and leave it here—with the earphone pressed up against the mouthpiece, and the switch on 'Conserve.' Next time we come we'll send out a message and the receiver will pick it up and bounce it back to us, and we'll go down along the direction."

·   ·   ·

Behind them lay the dead planet of Delta Trianguli. Paddy looked out ahead. "Adhil's next, then Loristan."

He picked up the key, scrutinized the letters on it. RXBM NON LANG SON.

He chewed his lip. "Now this is a different problem. On Alpheratz A and on Badau we at least knew which shebeen to buy at. But this time we have a key, and there's a million doors on Loristan, not to mention boxes, drawers, lockers, padlocks, jam cupboards—"

Fay said without raising her head, "It's not that difficult."

"No? And why not, pray?"

"Loristan is banker, broker, financier to the Langtry worlds. The Loristan Bank regulates currency for the entire galaxy and there's nothing like its deposit boxes for safety. They're so safe that not even the Sons of Langtry themselves could break into a box. And that's what the key is—a safe-deposit key."

"And why is this safe-deposit system so safe?" asked Paddy.

Fay leaned back against the bench. "First the central vault is encased in eight inches of durible and guarded by explosive mines. Then comes a layer of molten iron, then more durible and more insulation, then the vault. Second, the goods are banked mechanically, without human handling or knowledge.

"You go to the bank, buy a box, put in your valuables, take the key. Then you code the box with whatever arrangement of letters you wish and drop it in a chute. The machine carries it away, stacks it, and nobody knows where it is or which or whose is whose. The only records are in a big gelatine brain.

"To get your box, you go to any branch, punch your code on the buttons, insert your key and the combination brings you your box. Neither the key alone nor the code alone has any effect. The box holder is doubly protected against theft.

"If he loses his key or forgets the code then he must wait for the ten-year clearing, when all boxes which have laid undisturbed for ten years are automatically ejected."

"So," said Paddy, "all we do is drop down to Loristan, use the key and take off again?"

"That's all," said Fay. "Unless—"

"Unless what?"

"Listen." She turned on the space-wave. A voice spoke in the Shaul dialect. "All citizens of the cluster be on the lookout for Paddy Blackthorn and the young woman accompanying him, both Earthers. They are desperate criminals. Reward for their apprehension alive is a million marks a year for life, perpetual amnesty for all crimes, the freedom of the universe and the rank of Langtry Lord."

"They really want us," said Fay.

"Shh—*listen!*" And they heard the Shaul describe them in precise detail.

Another voice began to repeat the same message in Koton. Fay turned off the set.

"We're being hunted as Grover O'Leary hunted the white-eyed stag—with tooth, nail, and all odd angles."

Fay said, "I tried to make contact with Earth but there's still interference. No doubt the blockade is tighter than ever."

Paddy grunted, "And how about your Earther Agency then, that you train so exhaustively for and evidently serve with your every resource?"

Fay put on her faint smile. "Paddy, do you know I trust only three people in the world?" Myself, the chief of the Agency, and you? After all, the Agents are human. That reward would turn almost anyone's head. And all for a very small whisper."

"The fewer that knows, the better," Paddy agreed. He ran his hand through his hair. "Black-haired, they said. They must have caught Dr. Tallogg."

"Or maybe they tied together the Earther vandals on Alpheratz A and the inept performers at the Kamborogian Arrowhead."

"That sexy dance wasn't inept. You looked as if you had lots of experience."

Fay rose to her feet. "Now don't be so old-maidish. Certainly I have good coordination and I've had dancing lessons. Anyway, what do you care about my past? I'm not your type. You like those cow-eyed underslung Maeve women, remember? So much to squeeze, remember?"

"Ah, so I did," sighed Paddy, "but that was before I saw that smooth pelt of yours and now I'm tempted to change."

"Pish! I'm plain. Remember? With a skinny posterior. Remember?"

"Very well then," said Paddy, turning away. "Since you've the memory of the most revengeful elephant of India you're still plain and still skinny."

Fay grinned to herself. She said to his back, "We'd better try to change our appearances. There's hairwash and Optichrome in the locker. Maybe we'd better be blond for a while. We'll dye our clothes also. And I'm going to cut your hair short and wear mine differently."

Loristan was a small world and mountainous. Great forests of trees a mile high charged the air with oxygen, and a visitor's first experience with the low gravity and the oxygen produced a fine exhilaration.

Where the cities of Alpheratz A and Badau were low and severe Rivveri and Tham, the twin cities of Loristan, reared spectacular towers into the air. Buttressing planes of arched metal hung between, conquering space, sometimes for no other purpose than sheer exuberance. Raw rich color glowed everywhere. There was no gloom on Loristan, none of the Pherasic mysticism, the Badau stolidity. Here were bustle, aggressiveness, activity.

Paddy now had bright blue eyes and cropped blond hair. The combination lent him an expression of boyish naivete. He wore a blouse stamped with patterns after the Pendulistic school, loose breeches flapping at the ankles.

And Fay—where was the somber dark-haired girl Paddy had first seen? Here was a bright eager creature with white-gold elf-locks, eyes blue as frosty morning, strawberry mouth. And every time Paddy looked at her he groaned inside and the word Maeve came to be hated. Twice he tried to grab her and kiss her and twice she ducked and sprang across the cabin. Finally Paddy lapsed to a sullen indifference.

Loristan widened below, and the twin cities twinkled like jewels.

"Well," said Fay, "what'll it be? Shall we sneak down to a landing somewhere in the forest or use the public field, bold as life?"

Paddy shrugged. "If we tried slipping down out in the woods or in that Big Jelly Swamp they show on the chart there'd be a dozen guardboats on us like birds on a nutmeg. But when we pull into their public field they rub their hands and say, 'Fine, another couple of Earther savages to be fleeced,' and that's as far as their minds reach."

"I hope you're right," said Fay. She touched the

controls, the boat nosed down. They slipped quietly to a landing on the pitted field, settled among a dozen other boats of similar model. For ten minutes they sat, watching through the observation dome for any sign of undue interest.

No one seemed to heed them. Other boats took off and landed, and from one of the incoming ones a dark-haired Earther couple alighted. Coincidentally, the man wore a blue jumper.

Fay nudged Paddy. "Let's follow those two. If there's any suspicion, they'll certainly arouse it."

The two Earthers sauntered off the field and no one looked at them twice. With more confidence Paddy and Fay followed, through the terminal lobby and out upon the shining streets of Rivveri.

"There's the bank," said Fay, nodding at a spire of red marble shafted and splined with silver, "and there, see that counter along the side? That's the safe deposit. You need never even step inside."

Paddy said half to himself, "It can't be this easy."

"It can't be," said Fay. "I feel the same way. As if this city is wired like a big burglar alarm—a trap—and that red spire is nothing but bait for Paddy Blackthorn and Fay Bursill."

"It's a hunch I have," muttered Paddy. "A hunch that something is fishy."

Fay looked up and down the street with her new blue eyes. "Every hunch is supposed to have subconscious reasons for being."

"It's all too bright and open. Look at those butter-yellow Loristanese in the little pleated skirts, with their silly smiles on their faces and those sassy little caps. It's as if they're all nudging each other with their elbows, telling each other to watch the big joke when the axe falls on Fay and Paddy."

Fay squared her small shoulders. "Give me the key. All we can do is take a chance. After all we have two-fifths of the data and we could always bargain for our lives."

Paddy said gloomily, "You don't bargain in a nerve tube. You talk and gladly too. Those two sheets aren't safe till they're out of our hands."

"Well, we'll have to take the chance. Give me the key. You wait here and if anything happens go back to the ship, take off fast to Delta Trianguli, pick up the sheets, and get away with them."

Paddy snorted. "What do you take me for now? I'm thinking you're becoming too bold and independent with your ordering. It's me that'll go up there and draw the lion's tooth. There was never a Blackthorn yet that his woman did up the slops for him, and we won't ever start here out on this drunker planet Loristan."

"Boom—boom—boom," jeered Fay. "You sound like you're running for office." But she smiled and was evidently pleased. "Oh, let's both go. Then there won't be any argument and we can both feel virtuous."

With pumping hearts they marched up to the bench, found an empty booth. An armed guard stood at either end of the counter but paid them no heed.

Paddy pushed the key in the slot. Fay punched out the code on a set of buttons—RXBM NON LANG SON. Then came the wait. Ten seconds, twenty seconds—it was a paralyzed eternity.

A siren shrieked high on the red spire. The doors into the bank slid open, a pair of armed guards strode out toward the counter.

Paddy squared off. "Run, Fay—quick now. I'll hold 'em. They'll never take me alive. *Run*, girl! Get to the boat. You know where we've hid the stuff."

Fay giggled nervously. "You fool, shut up. It's lunch time. They're the relief guards."

A rattle, a click and a package fell into the hopper at their counter.

Fay picked it up, covered the green-and-orange medallion of the Loristan Langtrys.

"Now," she said, "back to the boat."

"They're watching us like hawks," hissed Paddy.

"Come along. You're acting like you've just robbed the bank!"

They walked briskly across the square, turned into the glass-fronted lobby, set out across the field. An armed guard ran toward them, shouted.

Paddy jerked around, put his hand in the pocket where he carried his little gun. "To the ship, Fay," he ground between clenched teeth. "Run, you've still got time."

"No," said Fay. "Wrong again. He's trying to tell us a boat is coming down on our heads."

Paddy, glancing up, saw the underside of a great excursion boat not two hundred feet above. They dodged swiftly out of danger.

There was their boat—the familiar little hull which had traversed so much emptiness, the observation dome through which they had seen so many stars.

"Inside," said Paddy. "Quick! Oh, there's a trap somewhere. I can smell it. They're trailing us to our boat and they've shorted out our drive." He ran to the controls, jerked the lift lever. "See? It's dead. No power."

"Of course not," said Fay. "The port is still open."

She slammed it shut. Paddy threw power to the jets, the boat lofted into the bright sky of Loristan.

"It *can't* be this easy," said Paddy, wiping sweat

from his forehead. "There must be some catch, some trick."

"It *can't* be this easy." Fay agreed watching from the side window. "But it is. No one is after us. No one even knows we've been here."

Paddy sank into a seat. "*Phew!*" he sighed. "It would be less strain on my poor tired nerves if we had a little trouble. Then I'd feel we had earned our loot."

Fay laughed, tossed the package to the desk, began to tear it open.

It was much like the other two. The first paragraph, like the one on the Pherasic sheet, dictated the spacing of the activation coils. The second paragraph detailed the time sequences for each of the five banks of coils. Then, as on the other sheets, there were two columns of three numbers apiece.

"We're off to Delta Trianguli and Angry Dragon Peak," said Fay. "And then to Almach and we'll see how the Shauls treat us."

IX

Almach lay to the right and below. Ahead hung the lurid face of Shaul. Paddy turned away from the telescope, spat in disgust.

"The first Langtry Son was a maniac when he picked this planet. It's like the hell old Father O'Toole predicted for me. I believe I'd rather raise my cottage in the shadow of the Angry Dragon."

"Shaul's very beautiful," Fay said mildly, "in a frightening sort of way."

"It's a yelling Satan's kitchen of a planet. Now see there—those orange spots. Are they volcanic craters or are they not?"

"They are."

"And those lava flows and steaming cinder heaps and the dust storms. How can men live on a planet like this?"

"They grow flaps of skin to protect their necks and to shield their faces," said Fay. "They develop a tolerance for acid in the air and don't feel easy unless they're mining the marvelous ores and jewels of Shaul."

"I've no flap of skin," growled Paddy. "I don't like acid and I don't like tunnels since the affair at Akhabats—though my ideas are not in demand. Now then, where are we heading?"

Fay said, "Corescens. The back wall. Irradiate with angstroms 685, 2590, 3001. Photograph!"

Paddy looked up, marveling. "And you remembered all those numbers?"

She twisted her lips in a bashful crooked grin. "I've got a good memory. And we're trained to use it in the Agency. It's easy to memorize numbers, once you know how."

Paddy made a long face. "And now you'll be telling me how you do it. Six eight five—add six and eight. That's fourteen; the one and four make five, and that's the third number. Also the one and four in one four four four. As for the last fours, they make eight, and since there's two of 'em, double it and that's sixteen. One from six is five, and there's your one four four four. Now as for two five nine aught—"

Fay said, "When you're done talking like an idiot, look up Corescens in the almanac."

Paddy thumbed through the Langtry Directory. "There's no Corescens listed."

"None?" asked Fay in a hurt voice.

"None. But we'll find it. And we'll need a camera and a means to deliver radiation at those frequencies."

"There's a good camera in that forward gear locker. Case Five, I think. We'll need respirators but we can get those at the space terminal and I suppose we can have a projector built for us at Aevelye."

"Correct. And now it's the hour's end. Let's hear the news."

Fay turned on the space-wave. A Shaul voice spoke from the mesh. "An official release from the capital has confirmed the rumors circulating the system for several weeks.

"Kolcheyou, Shaul Son of Langtry, together with the Sons from Alpheratz A, Badau, Loristan and Koto, were killed by an Earther pirate at the yearly council.

"The Earther, a convict by the name of Patrick Blackthorn, escaped and is the quarry of the most intensive manhunt in history. Reward for his capture reached unprecedented heights. There are hints that Blackthorn escaped with valuable space-drive information.

"The new Shaul Son of Langtry, Cheyonkiv Dessa, has announced that the mass assassination has created no emergency, that the fabulous rewards are offered merely to bring the Earth monster to justice.

"Blackthorn has been reported in hundreds of localities and each report is being carefully checked by local police. His last authoritatively known position was at Spade-Ace, Thieves' Cluster, in the company of a young Earther woman, name unknown. However there are other clues which the authorities will not publicize."

Paddy slumped back in the seat. "*Hah!* We're wanted, we're wanted bad!"

Fay said, "There's all space to hide in, a lot of little planets, a lot of big ones. For all anyone knows we might have taken off on a line and be clear out of the cluster by now."

Paddy grimaced. "I keep seeing a picture of us hanging by our heels from a post or kicking inside a nerve-suit." He wiped his forehead, ran his hand through his blond bristles. "It gives a man the value of his existence, this life of the hare and the hound. And never a priest to help you into the blessed life to come."

"Pish," said Fay. "Confess to me if you want to."

"Very well and why not? It's the intent that swashes a man's soul free of guilt. Now then, sister," and Paddy studied the bulkhead, "there was a sin which occurred on the planet Maeve but it's to be supposed I was sorely tempted.

"Ah, there's a green garden there at Meran—a terrace where men sit under plane trees and drink the soft mouth-filling peer of the place. Then those soft-eyed girls come swinging by with their shoulders and their long brown legs bare.

"They wear pearls in their navels and emeralds in their ears and when they look those long slow looks there's honey in a river between you and all the will for a decent Christian life flits away like gulls down the Bloody Foreland. Now then—"

Fay's face twisted in rage and disgust. "A confession? *Pah!* You're boasting!" She marched across the cabin. "The Shauls are right. Earther savages think of nothing but their glands."

"Now, now, my dear—"

"I'm not your dear! I'm an Earth Agent, worse luck, and if this weren't the most important thing in my life I'd turn around and head for Earth and put you as far out of my sight and mind as I possibly could!"

"Now, now, now. You don't know how lovely you look with your face all pink with rage."

Fay laughed bitterly. "Rage? Not on your life!" She strode to the galley and poured herself a bowl of soup, which she ate with crackers in moody silence.

Still turned away from Paddy she said, "We'll be landing in an hour or two."

Paddy interpreted the statement as an invitation to join her. Sitting down he chewed reflectively on one of her crackers.

"It's a sad responsibility for a pair of fallible humans...Now had we old Father O'Toole with us he'd go forth, take the data, hide all in his cassock, come back to the ship, and none would dare to interfere."

"Father O'Toole is far away," Fay pointed out acidly. "We must cope with this problem ourselves. Though I wish he were here and you were back in Skibbereen.... We've got a problem which you insist on ignoring. Shaul won't be like Loristan. They've got the brains of the system, the Shauls, and they're oversuspicious."

"Hmmm." Paddy frowned, drummed the table with his fingers. "If we were journalists when we set down we'd be allowed more freedom with our camera."

Fay said grudgingly, "You may be a lecher and a thief but you come up with an idea now and then."

They sat a moment in silence. Fay looked suddenly at Paddy with wide eyes. "We'll have to land on the central field, because there's no other.... We'll have to go through all that uncertainty again, only the Shauls are more careful and thorough. Suppose they take your psychograph?"

"Suppose they do?" said Paddy lightly. "Don't you know that I'm three different men? I'm Paddy Blackthorn, the Rapparee, and I'm Patrick Blackthorn, the pride of St. Luke's Seminary, who'll talk you the Greek and the Romish and the Gaelic till your ear shivers for the joy of it, and I'm Patrick Delorcy Blackthorn of Skibbereen, the gentleman farmer and horse raiser."

"There's also Paddy Blackthorn the great lover," suggested Fay.

"Right," assented Paddy. "There's four of me and a different psychograph for 'em all. So you see, I've three chances in four to confuse the suspicious devils."

"If you do you'll be the first. You can change your

fingerprints but you can't change your brain strenuata."

The Shauls had sheared off and leveled the peak of an old volcano to make Aevelye's space field. When Paddy and Fay brought their boat down they found themselves overlooking a vast panorama of badlands, a chopped and hacked region of red, yellow, and green-gray rock.

Directly below, a tremendous rift rent the planet, a chasm miles across and miles deep. Down one side, on a series of ledges, sat the city Aevelye—white buildings pressed against the walls of the gorge, facing out across the awesome valley.

As Almach sank, the light played on wisps of mist hanging in the valley on a level with the rim and the colors were like fantastic music—greens and lavenders, oranges, unbelievable pastels from the reflected and refracted light.

The boat came to rest on Aevelye Field—bare and quiet compared to the fields at Badau and Loristan. Fay shivered. "We can't help but be noticed."

Paddy looked out the dome. "Here they come—the Cossacks!" He patted Fay's shoulder. "The bold front, now, lass."

Four Shaul guards drove up to the ship in a jeep, jumped out. They wore tight sheaths of blue metallic cloth and three carried carbines slung over their shoulders. Their hoods of skin, which they held rigid and stiff, were stained red and painted with indications of rank. The officer, wearing a black star on his hood, climbed up the ladder, rapped smartly on the door.

Paddy opened for him without pumping clear the entrance lock and coughed at the acrid dust that followed the Shaul into the cabin.

The officer was a young man, very terse and exact. He pulled out a pad of printed forms. "Your papers, please."

Fay handed him the ship's license. The officer bent to look.

"Albuquerque Field, Earth." He looked up, turned to Paddy, scrutinized him up and down. "Name, please?"

"Mr. and Mrs. Joe Smith."

"Business and pleasure," Paddy replied jocularly. "We're tourists and journalists at the same time. We've been wanting to make the Big Line, and when we caught the news of the assassination we thought maybe we'd take some pictures around the planet."

The officer said without emotion, "Earthers are not in good reputation around the Five Planets."

Paddy protested. "Ah now, we're just working people and we've our living to make, whether there's births or deaths or war or peace. And if you'd say a good word for us we'd sure appreciate it."

The officer swept the interior of the craft with his eyes. "We don't have too many Earth journalists setting down at Aevelye in these small boats."

"Listen now!" said Paddy eagerly. "Then we're the first? There's been none from the Fax Syndicate—that's our competitor?"

"No," said the officer coolly. "You're the first." He returned to his printed form. "How long do you plan to stay?"

"Oh, maybe a week or until we accomplish our business. Then maybe we'll be on to Loristan or Koto for more."

"Ghouls," said the officer under his breath. He handed them an ink pad. "Your thumbprints please."

Gingerly they pressed their identities on his sheet.

"Now"—he wrote a moment—"here's a receipt and I'll have to take your power-arm and keys. Your boat is impounded. When you want to leave apply to Room 12, Terminal Hall, for a permit."

"Here now," protested Paddy. "Isn't this high-handed? Suppose we want to tour across the planet?"

"Sorry," said the officer. "There's a state of emergency, and we're bound to take precautions until things are normal again."

"Now then," Fay said nervously, "we don't mind a little inconvenience if we get what we want."

The officer was copying information from the ship's papers. At last he looked up, produced a pair of small flat boxes.

"Here are temporary respirators, which will serve until you buy permanent breathers. Now, please, if you will come with me there's a formality required of all Earthers."

"And what's that?" demanded Paddy truculently. "A return to the old closed-space system? I'll have you know I'm a citizen of Earth and Ireland too and—"

"I'm sorry," said the officer. "I merely obey orders, which are to pass all Earthers, no matter how innocent, through the psychograph. If you are not a criminal then you need not worry. If you are, then you will be accorded justice."

"The psychograph is not an instrument for innocent people," said Paddy. "Why, the indignity of it! I'll leave the planet first and spend my money on Loristan."

"Not now," said the officer. "I regret that these are emergency conditions and that certain hardships must be endured. Please follow me."

Paddy shrugged. "As you wish. I'll have you know, however, that I protest bitterly."

The officer did not reply but stood watching as Paddy and Fay donned their respirators. Fay's mouth drooped, her eyes were moist when they fell on Paddy. Paddy moved with sullen deliberation.

The officer gave them seats in the jeep, trundled them to a ramp leading to a hall under the field.

"Into Room B, please."

In Room B they found three other Earthers, two angry old women and a sixteen-year-old boy, waiting for their psychographs. One by one they were taken into an inner room to emerge a minute or so later.

At last the Shaul nurse beckoned to Fay. "You first, please."

She rose, patted Paddy's cheek. "I'm sorry it had to end like this," she said softly and disappeared.

A moment later the attendant motioned for Paddy.

Paddy entered a room, bare except for a desk, a chair, and a psychographer. A doctor stood waiting while an orderly in blue metallic military uniform sat by a desk watching a screen with a psychograph pattern pinned to a board beside it.

The doctor looked at Paddy once, then again searchingly. He turned to the orderly. "This one fits the physical data. The face is different, the hair and eyes are different but of course...Into the chair, please," he said to Paddy.

"Just a minute," said Paddy. "Am I a common criminal then?"

"That's what we are about to find out," the doctor told him quizzically. "In any event this is merely a routine check."

"What's all this?" Paddy motioned to the screen and the psychograph pinned up beside it—a pattern of lines like a weather chart superimposed on a relief map of the Himalayas.

"That, my friend," said the doctor imperturbably, "is the psychic pattern of Patrick Blackthorn—and if I may say so it's the oddest pattern I've ever seen. It's unmistakable.

"There's little chance of doing anyone injustice. Now if you'll take this seat and let me fit these pickups on your head...."

"I'll fit 'em," growled Paddy, taking a seat. He jammed the contacts down across his scalp. "Go ahead now and be damned to your bureaucratic nonsense."

The doctor snapped a switch. Paddy felt a slight tingling, a momentary drowsiness.

"That's all," said the doctor, glancing across to the orderly.

"Strange," muttered the orderly. "Come here, doctor..."

The doctor stared curiously at Paddy's pattern, shook his head. "Strange."

"What's strange?" asked Paddy.

"Your—ah, pattern. It's hardly typical. You can go. Thank you."

Paddy returned to the anteroom, found Fay pacing the floor nervously. She gave a small squeak. "*Paddy!*"

The attendant looked up sharply and Paddy's knees wobbled. Fay's eyes grew large and moist. She blushed red. Taking Paddy's arm she pulled him out into the big echoing lobby.

"Paddy," she whispered. "How did you get away? I was waiting with my heart in mouth, waiting for the shouting and banging—"

"Shh," said Paddy. "Not so loud, and I'll tell you a great joke. I was once in a battle and they lifted my scalp. The doctors sewed me up again with a big platinum plate across my sconce. I can laugh at those psychographs, because the metal shorts them all out and they never read the same on me."

Fay bristled like a porcupine fish.

"Why didn't you tell me?"

Paddy shrugged. "I didn't want to worry you."

"Worry—*Hah!* I'm only worried because now I'll have to live with you another couple of months."

"Now, now, my dear," said Paddy abstractedly. He took her arm. "And here is where we get our breathers."

X

Coming out of the terminal, they found themselves on a balcony hanging over Aevelye like an eagle's aerie. They stood in a bath of canary-yellow light and the sky over them had taken on an odd amber hue. Paddy and Fay crossed the balcony, stepped aboard an escalator which dropped them down, down, down to the white-columned city below.

They passed great residences perched on ledges, airy white houses set among the strangest vegetation of their experience. Stalks like stacks of tetrahedrons supported a foliage of crystalline spines or groups of olive-green slabs reticulated with slabs of red glass or flowers that were like an instantaneous photograph of an exploding opal—fragments held out from a center by invisible tendrils.

The buildings became of a more commercial character—shops displaying the richest wares of the universe, and presently Fay spied a sign reading TRAVELER'S HAVEN. They stepped off the escalator, walked along a trestle overhanging a thousand feet of clear space to a tall edifice of concrete waxy-green serpentine polished granite.

They entered, crossed to the desk. "We'd like lodgings," Paddy told the Shaul clerk.

The clerk flipped his hood casually, gestured to a small sign—EARTHER TRADE NOT SOLICITED.

Paddy tightened his lips, narrowed his eyes. "You skin-headed little run," he began. Fay clutched his arm. "Come, Paddy."

The clerk said, "The Earther hotel is down the slope."

Outside Paddy snapped, "Don't call me Paddy. I'm Joe Smith. Do you want them jumping on my neck?"

"I'm sorry," said Fay.

The Earther hotel was a gray block in the lower part of the city between two heaps of slag from a zinc refinery on the level above. The clerk was a wrinkled black-eyed Canope, crouching behind his desk as if he feared his guests.

"We want two rooms," said Paddy.

"Two?" The clerk looked from one to the other.

"My wife snores," explained Paddy. "I want to get a good night's sleep somewhere along the trip."

Fay snarled under her breath. The clerk shrugged. "Just as you like." He eyed Fay speculatively, handed them a pair of keys. "The rooms are dark and turned away from the view but it's the best I can do for you at the moment. Rent's a day in advance, please."

Paddy paid him. "Now we'd like some information. We're journalists from Earth, you see, and we're to take some pictures and we find our special lamp has come apart. Where can we have one made to our order?"

The clerk turned, punched a button, spoke into a

mesh. "Is Mr. Dane there? Send him across, please. I've got some business for him."

He turned back to his guests. "This is an old electrician that's down on his luck and he'll do it for you. Is that all?"

"Where and what is Corescens?" asked Fay.

"Corescens?" The clerk's mouth opened a little. He blinked uncomfortably. "You'll find it hard seeing Corescens—especially as you're Earthers. It's the dead Son's private residence out across the Fumighast Ventrole."

Dane hobbled in, a one-eyed skinny old man with a crooked neck, a long bent nose. "Yes, and what might ye be wantin'?"

Paddy said, "We need a special ultraviolet light source for our camera. It must have four separate units with variable frequency controls for each unit over the range six hundred to three thousand one hundred angstroms. Can you make it up?"

Dane scratched his pate. "It'll cost you dear, though. Three hundred marks."

Paddy drew back in indignation. "Faith, now. I'll use my flashlight first. Three hundred marks for a few bits of wire and junk?"

"There's my labor, lad, and my training. Long years now I've studied."

Two hundred fifty marks was the figure finally reached, delivery to be made in two days.

Darkness filled the valley outside like pale ink in a vast basin and the slope above was hung with a thousand colored lights—red, green, blue, yellow, all soft and vague as if their purpose were less to illuminate than to decorate.

On the terrace outside the hotel Paddy said to Fay, "Do you know, I can feel something of what the first

Son loved in this planet Shaul. It's as violent and queer as a madman's whims but the color and now the softness of the night are wonderful. And out there across the valley there's another settlement and the lights glow across to us like fireflies."

Fay said softly, "Is it nicer than Skibbereen, Paddy?"

"Ah!" sighed Paddy. "And now you've touched me, my dear. When I think of the turf smoke that they still burn after all these ages and how it comes recking in from the bog and the old pub around from where I was raised and the River Ilen—yes, I'll be glad to get home."

"Then there's always the terrace of Meran," suggested Fay, "with the beer and the women."

"Ah!" cried Paddy. "The beer, it's like the nectar of paradise and the girls with their soft hands! If you catch the pearl in their navels with your teeth, then they must do your bidding for as long as you will—that's the custom of Maeve—and some of them wear pearls as big as plums."

"If you'll excuse me," said Fay coolly, "I'm going to buy a map and find Corescens. I'll leave you to your reminiscences."

"Here now," cried Paddy. "Faith, I was but teasing. And you started me out on it!" But she had disappeared.

Next morning they took possession of a rough-steering old sightseeing platform—the proprietor of the rental yard had been reluctant to trust Earthers with anything better—and loading the camera aboard they shoved off and out across the hazy valley.

Paddy said, "And now where's Corescens that you studied on last night?"

"We've got to find Fumighast Ventrole," said Fay. "It's supposed to be twenty miles north, a dead crater."

They rose out of the valley into the blaze of Almach's light and the complex face of Shaul spread out to all sides.

Fay pointed. "See that smoke rising? That's the volcano Aureo and just beyond is Corescens."

Fumighast Ventrole was another vast chasm in the planet, nearly circular in cross section and so deep that its bottom could not be distinguished through the haze. The sides glistened and glittered, rays of light flashing and darting in a thousand directions like glass spears—back and forth, reflecting in sprays of pure primitive color, flickering, dazzling as the boat sank on snoring old jets.

As they reached the mouth of the gap there was a sudden *swushhhh* and a guard boat hung alongside.

"What's your business?" asked a Shaul with a black star painted on the inside of his hood.

"We're journalists from Earth and we want to photograph the home of the dead Son."

"Do you have a Decency Certificate from the Office of Rites?"

Paddy shoved his head forward. "Decency Certificate? Of course I'm decent, you insolent thrush! And I'll come aboard you in another minute."

Fay nudged him. "He means a permit. That's their way of speaking."

Paddy subsided with ill grace.

Fay said cheerily to the corporal, "No, we don't have any permit but all we want to do is take a few pictures."

The corporal said stiffly, "I'm sorry but—"

A Shaul in civilian dress, standing beside him, muttered into his hood. The corporal stared at Paddy intently, "When did you arrive?"

"Yesterday."

The corporal dialed a communicator, spoke at some length, nodded. He turned to Fay and Paddy.

"The orders are to let you down."

"Thanks," said Fay.

Paddy whispered, "The suspicious devils, they want to trap us and I'll bet you they watch us through telescopes all day."

Fay said, "It's a ticklish feeling—almost as if we're trapped in this hole."

"Hush now," said Paddy. "There's still the Black-thorn luck on our side."

Down into the glistening gap they saw that the walls were lined with great banks of crystals, hanging like bunches of grapes. As Almach rose in the sky, the colors glanced and twinkled, wove magic nets across the gap, tangled meshes of near-tangible fire. On a ledge a thousand feet below the surface sat a great house, a hall with two wide white-columned wings in a wide garden of the peculiar crystalline plants.

Swooping from nowhere the guardship drew alongside again.

"As a courtesy due journalists from Earth you have been extended freedom of the house. The bereaved family is not at home but the servants have been instructed to assist you. They will serve you what food and drink you wish."

He bowed with sardonic courtesy and the guardship rose swiftly as if it had been jerked up by a cable.

"Rats in a trap," said Paddy.

"Probably they don't suspect us directly," Fay said thoughtfully. "They think we might possibly be some sort of accomplices. They're giving us plenty of rope.

Well, we'll worry about it later. It's a chance we have
to take."

They landed on the terrace amid utter silence. The
cool space of the house opened in front of them and
through the columns they could see the rich furniture
for which the Shauls were famous—chairs of every
height and inclination, walls upholstered in peach-
colored floss.

There was no door, no glass—merely a curtain of
gripped-air to exclude insects and dust. It parted in
front of their faces with a slight sensation of bursting
as if they had walked through a soap bubble.

The majordomo bowed slightly and for the next
hour conducted them about the villa, answering their
questions but volunteering no information. Clearly he
considered the task beneath his dignity. Paddy and
Fay snapped pictures at random.

The area of interest for Paddy and Fay was the
terrace behind the house. Shielded from the poly-
chrome radiance of the chasm it was bathed in a soft
cool light from the sky. At the rear the cliff rose, faced
to a height of fifty feet with two-foot squares of aventurine quartz.

Involuntarily both counted three from the right,
two up. There it was, a clear yellowish slab, flecked
with a million flitting spangles.

A woman servant appeared to announce lunch
and the majordomo conducted them to a small
table set with synthetic fruits, a platter of toasted
fungus, yeast wafers, and rods of a porous dark
brown substance which crunched and tasted like
meat.

Paddy was gloomy. Twice he looked at Fay, started
to speak but was deterred by her warning frown. The
majordomo served them a light pink wine, which they

carried to the railing around the terrace, where they stood overlooking the gulf.

Fay said without moving her lips, "I feel as if every word is being picked up and broadcast to a desk where three or four Shauls are listening in dead silence."

"So do I," muttered Paddy.

Fay sipped her wine, stared across the color-shot emptiness. "We can't do anything more today."

"No, let's get back to Aevelye and our ship."

As they cleared the mouth of Fumighast Ventrole the guardship bellied down, pulled alongside, and the Shaul corporal requested the film pack of the camera for censorship purposes.

Glumly Paddy slid off the cartridge, handed it across the gap.

"It will be returned tomorrow," said the corporal.

Their ship had been searched. Nothing was out of place. Indeed the strongest indication of the search was a rather marked neatness to the cabin.

"Ah, the vandals!" Paddy ground between his teeth. "Now I wonder if—"

He met Fay's eye. She gave him such a brilliant glance that he subsided, and did no more than mutter under his breath.

For half an hour they spoke nothing but generalities. Then, with Almach settled in its flame of lavender and orange light, they left the boat, walked to the edge of the field, looked out across the great gorge, which was already filled with pastel shadows and glowing tendrils of mist.

Fay said, "They may *not* have the ship tapped for sound and there may *not* be a spy cell peeking at us somewhere—but as you know they're suspicious creatures and they're probably overlooking no chances. It seemed to me that their search job was just clumsy enough for us to notice and then start frantically after any secrets we might have had."

"Fay," said Paddy gloomily, "we're at a dead end. We're at a standstill. Any pictures we take they'll scrutinize with eyes like currycombs. If we try to bust down there with our ship, take our pictures and lambaste out again, they'll have us bottled up like the Green Imp of Ballycastle."

Fay, rubbing her chin with a pale finger, said nothing. Paddy felt a sudden surge of the protective instinct. Glancing down at the blond head beside him he wrapped an arm about her shoulders.

She said, "Paddy, I've got an idea...."

Paddy looked off into the night. "I've got one too."

She looked up quickly. "What's yours?"

"You tell me yours first."

"Well—you know that in all probability the Shaul data has been engraved or painted somehow in that aventurine quartz in a fluorescent dye which glows at the proper frequencies."

"Sure—of course."

"Presumably the whole wall glows—but only the single plate will have a legible message when illuminated by the particular four frequencies."

"Right."

"Tomorrow night we'll do some night photography—hundreds of shots."

"Ah," said Paddy, smiling whimsically down into her face, "and what a brain you hide behind that sober little face!"

She laughed. "Now, what's your idea?"

Paddy said with a stammer, "I want you to marry me, Fay."

"Now, Paddy Blackthorn," said Fay, "you don't

want to marry me any more than you want to marry that Shaul corporal."

"Ah yes, I do—and never say I don't," said Paddy energetically.

"Pooh, it's propinquity—animal spirits. A day ashore on Earth and you'll have forgotten all about me."

"Then you refuse me?" And Paddy narrowed his eyes.

Fay looked away. "I didn't say yes and I didn't say no. And I won't till after we're finished with this job and I see what kind of gentleman you are and how you conduct yourself when there's temptation in front of you.

"Now, Fay," said Paddy, squeezing her to him. "Then it's yes?"

Fay pushed him away. "It's a no—for now. And a maybe if I find you've stopped thinking about those Maeve women. How'd I feel with a home and two or three little Paddys and you pinching at all those Maeve girls' legs?

"Now enough nonsense," she said. "We've got the most important job that's ever been and all you talk about is Maeve women...."

"Just one little kiss," pleaded Paddy. "Just so that if the Shauls get us, I'll die happy. Just a little kiss."

"No—well, just one...oh, Paddy...All right now, get away from me or I'll dose your food until you won't know a woman from a barn owl."

XI

The next day was quiet. During the morning Fay pursued the ostensible purpose of their visit by making biographical memoranda concerning the life of the late Son at the Propaganda Office.

Paddy visited Dane, the electrician, and took delivery of the ultraviolet projector.

Dane was proud of his work—an aluminum case eight or nine inches on a side with a handle for carrying. Four lenses opened into the front, a power pack fitted into clips at the back. In a row along the top were four tuners with vernier settings, four output valves, four switches.

"And is it accurate," Paddy asked skeptically.

"Accurate?" cried Dane. "It's as accurate as the Interworld Standard that I calibrated it by! Three times I checked each one of the circuits and there's never an offbeat!"

"Good enough and here's your money with a bit of a bonus."

During the afternoon a messenger delivered the

prints to the pictures they had made the previous day. None was missing nor were there any deletions.

Evening came with its violent flare of color. Paddy and Fay stacked their equipment on the dilapidated old air-boat, rose over Aevelye, took off for Fumighast Ventrole.

Over the mouth of the hole the guardship pulled up alongside.

The same corporal saluted them, glancing at their makeshift equipment with contemptuous amusement.

"What is it now? More pictures? It's dark."

"We'd like to get some night shots," said Fay. "To get the effect of the lighting and the fluorescence of the rocks. We've brought along an ultraviolet projector."

"So *that's* why you had that thing built!" said the corporal. He shrugged. "Go to it."

They dropped away from him into the chasm. "'So *that's* why you had that thing built,'" Paddy mimicked in a girlish falsetto. "Strange he didn't ask when our wedding was to be—they seem so interested in all our doings."

They landed on the terrace in front of the house and the darkness, faintly luminescent, was like the fog of dreams.

Fay sighed. "If I weren't so scared and nervous I'd be in love with the place."

"Maybe we'll come here on our honeymoon," said Paddy. She peered at him through the darkness to see whether or not he was serious.

A voice at their elbow said, "Good evening." It was the Shaul majordomo. "More pictures?"

"More pictures is right," said Paddy. "We'd like some shots of you making the beds and maybe dumping the garbage down the chute or maybe putting away the famous silver."

"I'm sorry. I'm afraid that is impossible."

"In that case, with your permission we'll just infest the outer grounds."

"My permission has not been sought," replied the majordomo with a soft silken edge to his voice. "The orders to throw the grounds open to anyone who chose to drop in came from Aevelye."

Paddy grinned. "You and I now—we'd make a good pair on the stage."

The majordomo's cowl vibrated rapidly. He turned and walked off.

For an hour they took pictures of the villa and the silent garden, using a variety of ultraviolet frequencies. At last they worked their way around to the back terrace.

Paddy turned the projector against the back wall. It fluoresced beautifully in striking patterns of red, fiery yellow, gold, lemon-white. He played frequencies at random over the wall while Fay took pictures.

"Now, Paddy," whispered Fay. "The four."

Paddy set the dials. "Got the number of your films?"

"Yes. Three hundred six through three hundred nine, inclusive."

For a flickering instant Paddy pressed all four switches at once and in that instant the random glowings, lines, and loops in the significant square coalesced to form lines of legible characters. They even showed the same pattern as had the other data sheets—two preliminary paragraphs and two columns of figures.

"That's it," said Paddy. "Now—one at a time."

Using each frequency separately, they made four photographs.

"We'll make a few more," said Fay, "and then we'll go."

"Wonders of wonders," said Paddy. "I think we've got it."

When at last they rose above Fumighast Ventrole the guardship as before pulled up alongside and the captain requested the camera, the film pack and the ultraviolet projector.

"If the censor finds nothing wrong," he told them, "you'll have everything back tomorrow." Paddy and Fay flew back to their ship.

Again during the morning Fay noted information regarding the dead Shaul Son while Paddy, under the pretext of sealing a leak in the waterline, sought through the ship for spy cells without success.

During the early afternoon a messenger brought them their prints. Fay fanned them out swiftly—306—307—308—309. All there, clean and distinct. When superimposed they would spell out the Shaul fifth of the space-drive engineering.

"I'm off to Room 12," said Paddy. Trotting across the field to the Terminal Building he found Room 12 and recovered their power-arm and keys.

They filled water tanks, shipped two new energy cartridges. As Almach was dropping for its bath in the flaming evening vapors they took off. Presently Shaul was half of a bright orange globe below.

Paddy sighed. "Fay, I've lost ten pounds. "I've—"

"Shhh," said Fay. "We'd better check the ship for buttons and spy cells." In an hour, while Paddy encouraged her, she found two audio buttons disguised as rivets and a spy cell on the knob of a high locker.

"Now," she breathed. "Maybe we can talk—though I still feel jumpy."

Paddy rose to his feet. "And maybe there's time for a little kiss or two."

Fay sighed. "Oh, all right...Now stop it," she gasped. "*Stop* it, Paddy Blackthorn! You'd never marry a fallen woman and I intend to marry you honest and legal and make you squirm the rest of your life, so you behave yourself—until it's legal."

The boat drifted quietly in the great dark emptiness, as remote from the worlds of life as a soul after death. Paddy and Fay sat at the chart table in the observation dome, watching the far stars.

"It's only now," said Paddy, "with four-fifths of it behind us, that I'm getting the jitters."

Fay smiled wanly. She looked tired. Her eyes glowed with an unhealthy brightness, her skin was transparent, her fingers thin, nervous. "That's the way of anything, Paddy. If you're desperate any gain looks good. But now—"

"When I was chained on that little asteroid," said Paddy, "I could think of nothing finer than making off in that beautiful big-domed boat. Sure, I'd take any risk for it. There was nothing for me to lose. Now it's different. I want to live, I've something to live for." He looked at her with a glance that was like stroking her hair.

For several minutes they sat in silence. The boat drifted through space at an unknown speed. Perhaps it hung motionless. There was no way of knowing.

Paddy stirred. "See it out there—Mirach. It's staring back at us, daring us to come closer."

Fay's hand trembled. She laughed uncertainly. "It does have a funny look. Like one of the Koton eyes."

Paddy said, "Of all the Langtry races I hate only the Kotons."

"Probably because they've deviated the most."

Paddy shrugged. "I wonder. The Kotons and the Shauls resemble normal men the most of any. The Shauls have their skin cowls. The Kotons their saucer eyes."

"It's something beyond their mere appearance. It's their psychology. The Shauls are not too far removed from men. Earthers can understand most of their motives. But the Kotons—they're far away from any Earther's comprehension. It's as if they were stuff of their own twilight world.

"To speak to one you'd say here was the strangest most unique individual possible—a creature that might take to the wilderness to be alone with his own peculiarities. And then when you see them at one of their shoutings—"

"Or at a public torturing, like the time I was oiler on the *Christobel Rocket.*"

Fay winced "—then they're all the same and you can think of nothing but the rows and rows and rows of big saucer eyes. That's all you see. Acres of eyes as big as clamshells. And then you know that they're all the same in their oddness."

"Like a race of crazy people. But no," mused Paddy, "I'd hardly call them mad—"

"It would mean little if you did. They have so few sensibilities in common with the root stock."

"Few? There's not *any.*"

"Oh—there are a few. Curiosity—anger—pride."

"Well, that's true," Paddy conceded. "They're a cowardly crew, some of them, and they have those sex festivals."

Fay shook her head. "You're emphasizing the

wrong things. Their fear isn't the fear of Earthers. It's closer to what we'd call prudence. There's nothing of panic or fright in it, nothing glandular. And their sex is no more emotional than scratching an itch. Maybe that's their difference—the fact that their glands and hormones play such minor parts in their personalities."

Paddy clenched his fists, shoved out his chin. "I hate the vermin as I hate flies and I feel no more pangs killing Kotons than killing flies."

"I hardly blame you," said Fay. "They're very cruel."

"I've heard that they eat human beings and with relish."

Fay said mournfully, "And why not? Earthers eat pigs and that's about their attitude."

Paddy gritted his teeth. "They invented the nervesuit. What more can you say to their discredit?" He ran his fingers through his hair. "I hate taking you out there, Fay, and putting you to the risk."

"I'm no better than you are," she said.

Paddy rose to his feet. "In any case there's only nonsense in frightening ourselves. Maybe we'll have it easy."

Fay read from the last little piece of parchment. "'The Plain of Thish, where Arma-Geth shows the heroes to the wondering stars. Under my mighty right hand.' Do you know anything about Arma-Geth, Paddy?"

He nodded, turned to stare at the stars ahead. "It's a sort of heroes' memorial in the middle of the plain—'which may not be marred or imprinted on pain of sore death.'"

Fay stared. "And why do you say the last?"

"That's their law. It's a big plain, fifty miles square.

I'd say, and as flat as a table. They used a million Armasian and Kudthu and Earther slaves to lay it out level. There's not a bit of gravel the size of a pea to mar the flat. At the center of the plain are the great statues of all the old Sons. And Sam Langtry himself sits at the head of the aisle."

"You sound as if you've been there."

"Oh, not me. There's no one allowed near the plain but the Kotons and few of them. A drunken Shaul woman told me about it once."

Fay said dully, "You make it sound difficult."

"If we had an armed cruiser now," said Paddy, "we might drop smash down beside it, shoot up everything but what we wanted, take off before they could get to us."

Fay shook her head. "Not on Koto. There are five satellite forts covering every square mile on the planet. They'd have your cruiser broken and white-hot before ten seconds had passed."

"Oh, well," said Paddy, "I was just talking—letting my mind loose on wild schemes."

Fay frowned, bit nervously at her lips. "We've got to think of something. With four-fifths of the space-drive in our hands we can't allow ourselves to be captured."

"With or without as far as that goes."

They sat in silence a moment. Then Paddy said, "You'll drop me low and I'll parachute into the very center of Arma-Geth. In the dark I'll get our last sheet and I'll come out on the plain. There you'll drop by and pick me up once more."

"Paddy—are you serious?" Fay asked gently.

"Faith and how could I be otherwise? The very thought of the project raises the goose bumps on my neck."

"Paddy—you're too young to die."

"That I know," Paddy agreed. "That I know." He darted a glance across the gulf toward Mirach. "Especially on the public platforms."

"Just getting near the planet is dangerous," said Fay. "The forts detect anything coming down to Koto that's off the regular lanes. They're not free and easy like the other planets. And if we land at the Montras Field, we'd have to go through that examination again. Except that it probably would be a great deal more thorough."

Paddy pursed his lips. "If luck's with us we could make it past the forts."

"We can't trust to luck," said Fay. "We've got to use our brains."

"It's the old Blackthorn luck," Paddy reminded her. After a moment he added, "Of course it's the Blackthorn brains, too, which evens it up."

"Well, use them then!" snapped Fay. "Suppose when I dropped you down you were caught and they tortured everything you knew out of you? All about Delta Trianguli?"

Paddy screwed up his face. "Don't talk so. It takes away my heart for the venture."

"But suppose it happened for a fact? And we lost the four sheets? Then they'd have everything."

Paddy said, "Faith, I believe that if it came to seeing poor Paddy out of the nerve-suit or making sure of the space-drive you'd leave Paddy bellowing there like Bashan's Bull."

She inspected him as if from a distance. "Maybe I would."

Paddy shuddered. "Of all the millions of tender-hearted women in the universe it's you I went and picked out for a shipmate, one like the Hag of

Muckish Mountains, who sold her man to the devil for a goat."

Fay said coolly, "Control of space means a great deal to Earth. Right now those sheets are hardly safer than if we had them right here in the cabin. Neither one of us can risk being caught."

Paddy drummed the table with his fingers. "Now if we could only get them safe to the right people on Earth there wouldn't be this conflict and uncertainty and doubt between us."

"There's no conflict and doubt as far as I'm concerned," said Fay with a trace of bravado. "I love my life and I love you—no, now keep away from me, Paddy—but I love Earth and the old continents and oceans and the good Earth people more."

"You're an awful hard woman," said Paddy. "You're one of these fanatics."

She shrugged. "I don't think so at all. You feel the same way if you'd only stop and put it into words."

Paddy was not listening. He rubbed his chin, frowned. "Now I wonder—"

Fay said, "The Langtry ships around Earth are like bees around a honeycomb. Just hoping someone will try to smuggle the sheets to Earth."

"If we could only beam the information in on the space-wave."

"They'd jam us—and if we kept trying too long in one spot they'd triangulate and run us down." She rose and rubbed her hands nervously on the seat of her slacks.

"There's still another chance," said Paddy. "Celestrial Express, to Earth Agency."

"Mmmmmmmph. You're out of your mind."

Paddy reached for the Astral Almanac. "Not so fast, not so fast," he muttered. "The Blackthorn brain is a wonderful thing." He licked his finger, turned a page, searched down a column. "Pshaw! No deliveries being made this year."

"Will you stop being cryptic long enough to tell me what you're looking for?"

"Oh," said Paddy, "I thought there might be a comet cutting in from outer space close to Earth. Then we could include the sheets as part of the baggage. But there's nothing listed, nothing for another eight months."

Fay narrowed her eyes thoughtfully, said nothing. Paddy shrugged. "I guess we take our chances. There's still that old Blackthorn luck."

Oyster-white Koto hung below, Koto the twilight planet.

"It's a frightening place," murmured Fay. "So dim and dark."

Paddy essayed a confident laugh and was surprised at the shrill sound which left his mouth. "Now then, Fay, it'll go fast. One, two, three—down, up, off again, like old Finnigan at Bantry Station."

"I hope so, Paddy."

"Now we'll wait till those forts are spaced just enough to chance dropping our boat through."

Fay pointed. "There's a big hole out there over the Cai-Lur Quadrant."

"Down we go," said Paddy. "Now pray to Saint Anthony if you be a good Catholic—"

"I'm not," snapped Fay, "and if you'll give more mind to the boat and less to religion we'll gain by it."

Paddy shook his head reproachfully. "If old Father O'Toole would hear you, how he'd tut-tut-tut. Turn off the lights then and douse the field on the cowcatcher if we want to help our chances."

Koto bulged across their vision. "*Now!*" said

Paddy. "Off with all power and we fall like a dead rock and hope they're not too vigilant in the forts."

Ten minutes, twenty minutes passed. Silent and tense they sat in the dark cabin, their pale faces lit by the reflected glow of Koto.

The horizons spread, they felt the cushioning crush of air below them.

"We're past," breathed Fay. "We're down. Turn on the power, Paddy."

"Not yet. We'll get clear down into the traffic lanes."

The twilight surface of Cai-Lur Steppe rushed close. "The power, Paddy! Do you want to crash?"

"Not yet."

"*Paddy! Those trees!*"

A quick gust of power, a wrench of the rudder—the boat swooped belly-down, only yards from the surface, and charged hedge-hopping across the plain.

"Now then," said Paddy cheerfully, "and where's Arma-Geth from here?"

Fay pulled herself up into the seat. "You reckless idiot!"

"The lower we go, the safer," Paddy told her. "And Arma-Geth?"

She looked at the chart. "Magnetic compass one hundred fifty-three. About a thousand kilometers. There's a rather large city—Dhad—in our way. The traffic regulations for Koto—let's see." She flipped pages in *Traffic Regulations of All Worlds*. "Fourth level for us. Speed, two thousand KPH. If I were you I'd swing around Dhad."

Paddy shrugged. "On the fourth level we're just as safe over the town as over the country. Maybe safer if anyone has reported a strange space-boat."

Dhad swung below, a low city of flat wide roofs, glowing pearl-colored in the darkness, and presently was left astern. They crossed a range of mountains, rose to dodge Mt. Zacauh, a perfect cone eight miles high, slanted down across the Plain of Thish.

They dropped low, hovered, strained their eyes through the darkness. Paddy muttered, "It must be close."

Fay rose, "I'll tray infrared." A moment later, "I see it—about ten miles to the left. It looks quiet. You can drop down a little—there's nothing below us."

With the skids almost dragging, Paddy edged the boat toward Arma-Geth.

"About three miles," said Fay. "That's close enough. We don't know how well it's guarded or even if it's guarded at all."

Paddy set the ship down and the solid vibrationless ground felt curiously still, dead, silent, after the dynamic flight motion of the boat. Throwing open the port they put out their heads, listened. No sound, except for a soft distant chirring of insects. Three miles ahead, black on the gray luminescence of Koto's sky, rose a confused group of silhouettes.

"Now," said Paddy thickly, "my tools, my gun, my light. I'll be out there and back in less time than you'll know."

She watched him strap on his equipment. "Paddy—"

"What now?"

"I should be coming with you."

"Perhaps you should," Paddy agreed easily. "And if so I'll come back for you. But right now it's only a reconnaissance I'm making and you're the rear guard. Unless of course the stuff is there for the taking, so ridiculously easy that I can't resist it."

"Be careful, Paddy."

"Indeed I will, you can count on it. And you mind

for your own safety. Be ready to jump if it gets dangerous. If there's any shooting or disturbance—don't wait for me."

He dropped to the ground, stood listening. *Chirr, chirr, chirr*—a sound like a billion tiny bells.

Paddy started briskly for the silhouettes, treading the smooth swept surface of the plain. The silhouettes grew, towered past the gray afterglow, loomed up to the stars. There was no sound, no hint of movement, no lights. More slowly he advanced, ears and eyes like funnels.

He came to a stone wall, cold and moist, high as his head. He felt along the top, grasped the edge, hauled himself up. He was on a great stone pavilion. To either side rose dark statues—the Koton Sons of Langtry, row after rigid row, conventionalized, sitting in low chairs, staring with wide mother-of-pearl eyes across the sacred Plain of Thish.

Paddy sat a moment quietly, listening, every nerve in his body alive, groping for sensation. He rose to his feet, moved across the stone to the nearest statue. Where was the latest? Logically it should be the last statue of the series at the end of a row.

He felt along the base of the statue nearest him, looked along the sides, saw in faintly luminescent letters—*Lajory, 17th Son of Langtry*. Following it was a series of dates and ceremonial phrases.

He must be close, thought Paddy. The late Son was the nineteenth of the line. To his ears came the shuffle of footsteps on the stone. He clapped his hand to his gun, froze.

A pair of dark figures passed thirty feet away. There was the milky flash of great night-seeing eyes and they were gone. Had they seen him? Paddy pondered. They had seemed neither surprised nor startled. Perhaps they had mistaken him for a devotee. Best to make haste in any event.

He moved to the next statue. *"Golgach, 18th Son of Langtry,"* read the plaque.

To the next, *Ladha-Kudh, 19th Son of Langtry.* Here was his goal with the fifth sheet under the right hand. The hand lay on the knee, palm downward. Paddy looked up. Twenty feet. He took a last look around. No sight, no sound, no one to watch for thieving intruders.

He set his toe in a cleft, heaved himself up on the pedestal. The shuffle of steps—Paddy flattened against a pillar of the great chair. The sound passed.

Heart thumping Paddy hauled himself up the side of the chair into Ladha-Kudh's lap. Above loomed the stern dish-eyed face of the man he had killed and to Paddy's excited brain, the mother-of-pearl plates that were the eyes seemed to stare down accusingly.

Paddy grimaced. "Now's the time for the banshee to howl if ever he's going to. Ah, bless the Lord, may the creature's ghost still prowl the asteroid where he was killed."

Paddy crawled out the right leg to the hand, felt the stone fingers. "Now how will this be?" thought Paddy. "Will they raise up easy-like or will I want a charge of jovian powder to lift the hand away? First we'll try my bar."

He unhooked the pry-bar from his belt, pushed it under the hand, applied force. *Snap!* The ball of the thumb broke off, fell clattering to the pavement.

Paddy crouched, tingling all over. No sound—he felt at the fractured part, sensed the beginnings of a cavity. Bringing up his flashlight, he directed the tiniest whisper of light possible at the broken spot. A cavity it was and Paddy eagerly plied the bar.

A stern voice came from below. "What are you doing up there? Come down or I'll pick you off with a beam."

Paddy said, "Right away. I'm coming." He reached into the cavity, pulled out a metal box, shoved it into his pouch.

"Come down!" said the voice. "By the justice of Koto come down!"

Paddy slowly crawled back to Ladha-Kudh's lap. Trapped, caught red-handed—how many of them were there? He peered toward the pavement but could see only darkness. But they could doubtless see him well with their big twilight eyes.

He let himself down the leg of the chair. If he could only see. He snatched his light, flashed it along the ground. Three Kotons—uniformed, guns at ready— and they were dazzled. Paddy shot them—one, two, three—left them thrashing on the stone. He jumped down, hit with a jar, rose, raced to the edge, dropped over to the Plain of Thish.

He paused an instant, listened. He heard his own panting. The darkness bulked heavy with menace but he dared not use his flash. Above him he heard movement, staccato voices, sounds of anger.

Crouching, he scuttled off across the plain. At his back came a shrill whistle and over his head he heard a throb, a hum.

Paddy dodged, ran with mouth open, eyes staring into the gloom. Oh, to be in the ship! Fay, Fay, have the port wide!

A thud ahead of him, a swarm of figures. Paddy shot wildly, kicked, punched. Then his gun was wrenched away and his arms seized.

XII

There was no talk. With swift efficiency they trussed him with many folds of sticky tape, rolled him onto the floor of the air-boat. It rose, took him through the sky.

Night ebbed. The dim twilight that was Koto's day stole upon them like cool water. Paddy lay on the floor between two benches. Four Koton guards watched him with quiet expressionless eyes.

The boat landed. They laid hands on him, bore him across a square. Paddy glimpsed a tall spidery structure off in the distance, knew it for the Montras Traffic Control. He was in Montras.

Kotons moved past without interest and a small party of Alpheratz Eagles craned their necks. The Kotons walked with an odd loose-kneed gait like comedians mimicking secrecy. They had thick pale hair, growing straight up like candle flames. The soldier clans wore their hair shorn on a plane an inch above their heads and one man on Koto shaved his head—the Son of Langtry.

Across the square to a large blank-walled building

Paddy was carried and here the party was joined by other guards in short black uniforms cut and scalloped in eccentric half-moons.

They took him through a dark hall, smelling of carbolic acid, into a room bare except for a table and a low chair. They laid him on the table and departed, leaving him by himself. He sweated, tugged, wrenched mightily at his bonds without success.

A half-hour passed. A Koton in the regalia of Councillor to the Son entered the chamber. He stepped close to Paddy, peered into his face.

"What were you doing at Arma-Geth?"

"It was a bet, your Honor," said Paddy. "I was after a souvenir to show my friends. I'm sorry now I committed the misdemeanor, so if you'll untie me I'll pay the fine and go my way."

The Councillor said to a corporal behind him. "Search this man."

He looked at Paddy's equipment, picked up the metal box, glanced at Paddy with opalescent fire in his eyes, turned, left the room.

An hour passed. The Councillor returned, halted beside the door with a bowed head. "Zhri Khainga," he announced. The guards bowed their heads.

A Koton with a polished bald head entered the room, swung across to Paddy.

"You are Blackthorn the assassin."

Paddy said nothing.

The twentieth Son of Langtry put a quiet question. "What have you done with the other material?"

Paddy swallowed a lump in his throat the size of an egg. "Now, my lord, let me loose, and we'll talk the situation over as one man to another. There's rights and wrongs to everything and maybe I've been over-hasty time and again."

"What have you done with the rest of the data?" asked Zhri Khainga. "You might as well tell me. It will never do you or your planet any more good since now we possess a crucial segment of the information."

"To be perfectly frank, Your Honor," said Paddy ingenuously, "I never had anything else."

The Son turned, motioned. From a cavity in the wall they pulled a machine that looked like a heavy suit of armor, lifted Paddy, laid him inside. One bent down, deftly taped Paddy's eyelids open, then the cover was closed on him. Instantly every inch of his skin began to tingle faintly as tiny fibrils sought and joined to each of his nerve-endings. In front of his taped-open eyes a hemispherical screen glowed.

He saw moving shapes, a dingy flickering of low fires. He was looking into a stone-vaulted room with a stained floor. Ten feet away a man stood impaled. Paddy heard his screaming, saw his face.

The guards turned, looked at him with great blank eyes. He saw them reaching, felt their hands, the actual clutch at his wrists, under his knees. It was reality. The fact of the screen, had left his mind.

They knew the art of stimulating numb minds. They had perfected torture to the ultimate. Past-thought pain might be inflicted time and again with no harm to bone or body. A man could live his entire life in sensation.

And presently the operators would know their subject. They would discover how to grind out his sickest shrieks and the pattern would be elaborated, adjusted, embroidered to a delicate vortex.

Time would become elusive, the world would be vague and strange. The nerve-suit would be reality and reality would be the dream.

A voice gonged at Paddy. "What did you do with the other data?"

It was a sound from a tremendous brazen throat, without meaning. Paddy could not have answered had he wanted to.

After a period the question was no longer asked and then it seemed as if the torture had become meaningless.

Paddy emerged from quiet suddenly with a clear vision. The face of Zhri Khainga looked down at him.

"What did you do with the remaining data?"

Paddy licked his lips. They wouldn't trick him. He'd die first. But there was the rub! This kind of torture didn't let a man die. One twentieth of such treatment would kill a man were it fixed on him the normal way! Here they could torture him to death as many times as they chose and bring him back fresh and sound, nerves tingling and keen for the next session.

"What did you do with the other data?"

Paddy stared at the pale face. And why not tell them? Space-drive was lost to Earth in any event. Four-fifths was as bad as none at all.

Paddy grimaced. Suggestion from without. It must be, since this was the Son's own arguments. Fay! He wondered about Fay. Had they caught her, had she got away? He tried to think but the nerve-suit left him little leisure.

"What did you do with the other data?"

Zhri Khainga's head was close, his eyes dilated, and his face was like a death's-head. The eyes dwindled, expanded again. Wax, wane, swell, subside. Paddy was having visions. The air was crowded with old faces.

There was his father Charley Blackthorn, waving

a cheery hand at him, and his mother, gazing from her rocking chair with Dan, the collie, at her feet. Paddy sighed, smiled. It was beautiful to be home, breathing the turf smoke, smelling the salt fishy air of the Skibbereen wharves.

The visions flitted and danced, swept past like the seasons. The jail at Akhabats, the asteroid, the five dead Sons of Langtry. A quick flitting of scenes like a movie run too fast. There now, something he recognized—Spade-Ace. The doctor and Fay—Fay as he had first seen her, a small dark-haired imp of a girl. And beautiful—ah! so beautiful!

The grace in her movements, her lovely dark eyes, the fire in her slender body—and he saw her dancing at the Kamborogian Arrowhead, her rounded little body as soft and sweet as cream. And he had thought her plain!

He saw her with her golden hair, with the new arch side glances she had begun to give him. But now her eyes were full of bright anger and pity.

"What did you do with the other data?"

The wraiths departed regretfully. Paddy was back in the bare room with the Koton Son of Langtry, who wanted to know the secret of space-drive, the secret his grandfather twenty times removed had stumbled upon.

Paddy said, "Ah, you ghoul, do you think I'd be telling you? Not on your life."

"You can't resist, Blackthorn," said the Son mildly. "The strongest wills break. No man of any planet can fight indefinitely. Some last an hour, some a day, some two days. One Koton hero stayed two weeks and held his tongue. Then he spoke. He babbled, craving for death."

Paddy said, "I suppose you gave it to him then?"

Zhri Khainga made a quick quivering motion with his mouth. "Then we took our revenge on him. Oh, no. He still lives."

"And when I speak—after that you'll take your revenge on me?"

Zhri Khainga smiled, a ghastly grin that affected Paddy's viscera. "There is yet your woman."

Paddy felt flat, buffeted, overpowered. "You've—caught Fay then?"

"Certainly."

"I don't believe it," said Paddy weakly.

Zhri Khainga tapped an upright tube on the table with his shiny blue-gray fingernail. It rang. A Koton in a yellow breechclout scuttled into Paddy's range of vision. "Yes, Lord, your magnificent commands."

"The small Earther woman."

Paddy waited like a spent swimmer. Zhri Khainga watched him carefully for a moment, then said, "You have a projective identification with this woman?"

Paddy blinked. "Eh, now? What are you saying?"

"You 'love' this woman?"

"None of your business."

Zhri Khainga made play with his fingernails on the tabletop. "Assume that you do. Would you then allow her to suffer?"

Paddy said quietly. "What would be the difference since in any event you'll torment us till you tire of the sport?"

Zhri Khainga said silkily, "Not necessarily. We Kotons are the most direct of all intelligences. You have put me in your debt by killing my father, thus setting me free to shave my head. Life and death are mine. Now I have overpower. I rule, I direct, I envision.

"Already two hundred of my jealous brothers are stacked in the Cairn of South Thinkers. If you helped

me to sole knowledge of the space-drive over the false
Sons from Shaul, Badau, Alpheratz, and Loristan—
then there would be an unbalance indeed."

Paddy said. "Now butter won't melt in your mouth,
I don't understand you. You are bargaining with me?
What for what? And why?"

"My reasons are my own. There is dignity to be
considered."

"And haste?" suggested Paddy.

"Haste—and you might lose your memory. That is
common when a man lies too long in the nerve-suit.
The imagination begins to intrude upon fact and
presently information is untrustworthy."

Paddy crackled a wild laugh. "So we've got you in a
corner! And your nerve-suit won't get you your bacon
after all. Well, then, old owl, what's your bargain?"

Zhri Khainga stared expressionlessly across the
room. "On the one hand you may return to Earth, with
your woman and your space vessel. I crave the death
of neither of you."

Zhri Khainga flicked with the back of his hand.
"Negligible. Riches, money? As much as you desire."
He flicked again. "Negligible. Any amount and I will
not say no. That on the one hand. On the other—"

A sound interrupted him. Paddy turned his head
sharply. It came from a nerve-suit which had been
quietly rolled into the room—a cry of desperation,
contralto, aching, lost.

"That," said the Son of Langtry, "is your woman.
She is experiencing unpleasantness. That is the
alternative—for both of you. Forever and ever for all
your lives."

Paddy struggled to rise but was afflicted by a
strange weakness as if his legs were muscled with
loose string. Zhri Khainga watched attentively.

Paddy said hoarsely "Stop it, you devil—you devil!"

Zhri Khainga made a sign with his hand. The Koton in the yellow breechclout snapped down a bar. A sigh, a gasp came from within.

"Let me talk to her," said Paddy. "Let me talk to her alone."

Zhri Khainga said slowly. "Very well. You shall talk together."

XIII

"Fay, Fay, Fay!" cried Paddy. "Why didn't you leave the wretched world when you had the chance?"

She smiled wanly. "Paddy, I couldn't leave you. I knew I should. I knew my life was more important to Earth than to you. I knew all the things that the Agency drilled into me—but still I couldn't leave without trying to help. And they trapped the ship."

They stood in a wide concrete hall, a hundred yards long, high-ceilinged, illuminated with a glow that seemed blue and yellow at the same time, like strong moonlight.

Paddy looked in all directions. "Can they hear us now?"

Fay said dully, "I imagine that every sound we make is amplified and recorded."

Paddy moved close, and said softly into Fay's ear, "They want to trade us our lives."

She looked at him with wide eyes that still held traces of terror. "Paddy—I want to *live!*"

Paddy said between his teeth. "I want you to live too, Fay—and me with you."

She said desperately, "Paddy, I've thought the whole thing out. And I don't see what we gain by holding our tongues. The Kotons will get the space-drive—but what then?

"Earth wouldn't have it in any event since we've got only four fifths. And the four fifths"—she breathed in his ear in a whisper so low he could hardly hear—"I can dictate from memory."

"From—" Paddy gasped.

"Yes. I told you once I was trained for that."

"Hmmm."

Fay said softly, "If we were able to keep silent no one would have space-drive. In ten years there'd be no more star travel. On the other hand, if we told what we know—and if we can get back to Earth—then Earth will have as much as we have now."

"Which is as good as nothing," Paddy said bitterly. "Of the thirty numbers you only know twenty-four. Twenty-four dial settings."

He paused, blinked. A picture came to his mind from a past that seemed remote as ancient Egypt. It was the interior of the manifolding shop on Akhabats, where the five Sons came to curl power into the tungsten cylinders. Five panels, each with three dials.

"Fay," said Paddy, "I'm not fit to live."

She looked at him in alarm. "What's the matter?"

Paddy said slowly, "I see it all now and I see it clear. We've been abysmal fools. I've been the worse one. Now on these sheets"—he leaned to her ear—"remember the duplications?"

"Oh, Paddy?"

He said, "When I broke into that shop on Akhabats I saw a curling machine. There were fifteen control knobs. Those data sheets show six readings to a sheet—thirty in all. Does that mean anything?"

She nodded. "There are duplicates of the numbers too. Paddy—we had it all!"

"*All* of it," said Paddy. "We didn't need to come to Koto any closer than the Southern Cross."

Fay winced.

"We've got to get away," said Paddy with great energy. "Somehow. Because in that little cap of yours you've got space-drive."

Fay shook her head sadly. "They won't let us go, Paddy. Even if we tell everything we know they'd still kill us."

"Not till we'd blown the fuses in all their nerve-suits."

"Oh Paddy! Let's think—*think!*"

They thought. Paddy said, "He's hot after us, that Zhri Khainga, he's got the wind up. But why? Maybe word has got out to the other planets that he's caught us and all the spies and agents and secret services are going into action and he doesn't want to chance our holding out till the others get to see us."

There was a moment of silence. "Think," muttered Fay.

"Listen here," said Paddy. "We'll tell him that you'll go out to get the sheets and I'll stay as a hostage. Then you go to Earth and we'll spring the news that we know all there is to know about space-drive. Then you buy me back for twenty space-drives more or less."

"At the going rate," said Fay dryly, "that's twenty million marks. Are you worth that much?"

"That's the best I can think up," said Paddy. "There's no other way of getting us both out alive and the drive to Earth."

"Zhri Khainga won't like it," said Fay. "He'll want us to trust him. After he gets the sheets—*then* he turns us loose."

"I wonder," said Paddy.

"What?"

"Could it be that he'd agree to all of us going? We'd take him to you-know-where alone—and there we'd switch."

Fay said breathlessly, "It would be fair that way and he'd be getting the quick action he seems to want. Let's ask."

Stepping gingerly past the ranked crew members, conscious of the oyster-colored gaze, Paddy and Fay entered the familiar cabin which had taken them so far.

Zhri Khainga followed them, the port was slammed shut, they were cast adrift from the mother ship. Paddy and Fay stood stiffly, silently by the control deck; Zhri Khainga took a seat back in the cabin and leaned back at his ease.

"Now," he said, "I have complied exactly with your conditions. Here is your space-boat—we are alone. Take me to the hiding place of the data, I will call my own vessel, you may leave me and go your way in friendship. I have done my part. See to it that you keep good faith."

Paddy looked at Fay, rubbed his nose uneasily. "Well, now, to tell the truth, we'd like to look the ship over. Some of your men—by mistake, I'm saying— might be asleep in the bilges or checking stores in the forward locker."

Zhri Khainga nodded. "By all means satisfy yourselves. In the meantime," he turned to Fay, "perhaps you will put your ship on course."

Wordlessly Fay climbed up into the seat, threw the boat into space-drive and the vessel which had brought them from Koto twinkled an enormous distance astern.

Paddy came back. "Nothing," he grumbled. "Not hair nor hide."

Zhri Khainga nodded his head sardonically. "It troubles you that I keep to the terms of the bargain?"

Paddy muttered under his breath. Fay sat looking into the blank outside the port. Suddenly she pulled back the space-drive arm. The boat surged and sang into normal continuum once more."

"Look outside, Paddy," she said. "Around the hull."

"That's it," said Paddy. He pulled an air-suit from the rack, stepped in, zipped up the seam, set the bubble on his head while Zhri Khainga watched without words.

Paddy vanished outside the lock and Fay waited beside the controls, covertly eyeing the Koton, trying to fathom the weft of plot and plan below the dome of the shaven pate.

"I am thinking," said Zhri Khainga, "of great deeds. The wealth of any imagining shall be mine. I will give a quadrant of the planet to the plain of Arma-Geth—it shall be extended.

"Mountains will be leveled, the plain will be floored with black glass. So shall the statues dwell in the opulent silence and there will be my magnificent entity among them. I shall be magnified a thousand times. For all eternity will I tower—mine will be the life-loved pivot of history."

Fay turned, looked out through the port. Where was Sol? That faint star? Perhaps.

Paddy entered the ship. Another figure followed him. In the bubble Fay saw the great-eyed head of a Koton.

"This is what I find strapped to the hull. Do you call that subscribing to our proposals?"

Zhri Khainga sat upright. "Quiet now, little man! Who are you to challenge my wishes? You should be glorying in your fortune, that you give freely what otherwise could be wrung from your lips." He sat back in his chair. "But now—we are committed."

The Koton who had entered the ship with Paddy had not moved from his position. Zhri Khainga waved his fingers. "Out. Fly through space with your hands. You are not needed."

The Koton hesitated, looked up at Fay, back at the Son of Langtry, slowly turned, let himself out the lock. They saw him push himself away from the ship and drift off alone and hopeless.

"Now," said Zhri Khainga, "are you satisfied? We are alone. To the hiding place. Please be swift. There is much of importance awaiting my pleasure throughout the universe. Note that my gun is at hand, that I shall be alert."

Paddy slowly joined Fay on the control deck. "Go on, Fay. Set the course."

Delta Trianguli shone far and cold to the left. The dull black planet bulked below. Zhri Khainga, at the port, said, "Delta Trianguli Two; am I right?"

"You are," said Paddy shortly.

"And now where?"

"You'll see in due course."

Zhri Khainga wordlessly seated himself once more.

Paddy went to the transmitter, sent out a call on the frequency used in the air-suit headsets. "Hello, hello."

They listened. Faintly came, "Hello, hello," out of the receiver.

Zhri Khainga moved uneasily. "There are others here?"

"No," said Paddy. "None but us. Did you get the line, Fay?"

"Yes."

The dead face of the planet passed below— plains flat and dull as black velvet, the pocked mesh of mountains, which looked as if they had been dug by monstrous moles. Dead ahead rose an enormous peak.

"There's Angry Dragon," said Fay.

She set the ship down on the plain of black sand. The hum of the generator died, the ship was still.

Paddy said to the still seated Son of Langtry, "Now listen close and don't think to trick us, for sure you'll never win by it. You might get our lives but you'd never hold the four sheets for your own."

The Koton stared unblinking.

Paddy continued. "I'm going out there, and I'm going for the sheets. They're well hid. You'd never find them."

"I could have a hundred thousand slaves on this spot next week," observed the Koton tonelessly.

Paddy ignored him. "I'll get the sheets. I'll lay them on that bit of black rock out there. Fay will stay here in the ship. When I set them down you'll call your ship, tell them where to come for you, where to pick you up.

"Then you'll get in your air-suit and come toward me and I'll leave the sheets and go to the ship. When we pass each other you'll put down your gun and go on. I'll continue toward the ship and so we'll take our leave. You'll get the sheets and in a day or so your ship will be here to take you home. Is that agreeable?"

Zhri Khainga said, "You allow me little scope for tricking you. You are strong and muscular. When I put down the gun what is to prevent you from attacking me?"

Paddy laughed. "That little poison ball-whip you carry along your arm. That's what I'm afraid of. What's to keep you from attacking me?"

"The fact that you can outdistance me by running, and thus regain your boat. But how will I know that you are not giving me bogus data sheets?"

"You have binoculars," said Paddy. "I'll hold the sheets up for your inspection and you can watch me put them down. They're unmistakable—and with those binoculars you can read every bit of the text."

"Very well," said the Koton. "I agree to your conditions."

Paddy slipped into his air-suit. Before setting the bubble over his head he turned to the seated Koton. "Now this is my last word. By no means try to trick us or catch us off guard.

"I know you Kotons are devils for your revenges and your tortures and that you love nothing better than blackhanded treachery—so I'm warning you, take care or it will go ill with you and your hopes."

"What is your specific meaning?" inquired the Koton.

"Never mind," said Paddy. "And now I'm going."

He left the ship. Fay and the Koton could see him through the dome, marching across the black sand toward the peak. He disappeared into the tumble around the base.

Minutes passed. He reappeared and Fay saw the glint of the golden sheets.

Paddy stood by the black rock, held the sheets up, face toward the space-boat. Zhri Khainga seized his binoculars, clamped the funnel-shaped eyepieces over his eyes, stared eagerly.

He put down the binoculars.

"Satisfied?" asked Fay brittlely.

"Yes," said the Koton. "I'm satisfied."

"Then call your ship."

Zhri Khainga slowly went to the space-wave transmitter, snapped the switch, spoke a few short sentences in a language Fay could not understand.

"Now, get out," said Fay in a voice she could hardly recognize as her own. "You keep your part of the bargain, we'll keep ours."

"There is much yet unsaid," the Koton murmured. "The tale of your insolences, your detestable audacities."

Fay's body surprised even herself. Without conscious volition she sprang at Zhri Khainga, snatched the gun. It was hers. Clumsy now, juggling it, fingers shaking, she jumped back. Zhri Khainga gasped, leaned forward, flung out his arm. Poison-filled balls on elastic strips swished an inch from Fay's face.

"*Ahhh!*" she cried. "Get out, now—get *out!* Or I'll kill you and gladly!"

XIV

Zhri Khainga, his face a strange pasty lavender color, assumed his air-suit. Menaced by his own gun, he backed out of the boat.

Paddy had been waiting. Now he stepped forward and the Koton ran out to meet him, bounding, hoping, peculiarly agile.

Paddy met him halfway. He paused, expecting the Koton to throw down his gun. The Koton ran past, aching for the golden sheets. Paddy hesitated—then, seeing no gun at the Koton's belt, turned and ran for the boat.

Fay let him in, Paddy pulled off the head-bubble, looked at Fay's tense white face. "What is it then, Fay?"

"There's no power."

Paddy's shoulders sagged and his hands paused at the zipper of the air-suit. "No power?"

"We're marooned," she said. "And that Koton ship will be here in a few days—maybe less." She stepped up on the deck, looked out the dome toward the Angry Dragon. "And Zhri Khainga is waiting."

157

"Och," muttered Paddy. "We'd walk out across that black sand and give up our breaths first." He joined her on the control deck. "Are you sure about the power now? I was fooled once myself." He tried the controls. They were dead.

Paddy chewed his lip. "That villain worked some sort of relay switch into the drive, that would cut off our energy once we landed. And how he must be gloating!"

"Now he's got the sheets," said Fay, "and he can hide from us until his ship comes. We could never find him."

"It's rats we're like, on a sinking ship. Try the space-wave, Fay! Send out a call."

She flipped the switch. "Dead!"

Paddy shuddered. "Don't be using that word so much." He paced, two steps across the deck to port, four steps back to starboard, back to the center of the cabin. "Now try the anti-gravity. That's on its own special unit and there's no connection."

Fay slid the metal boss. Their weight left them.

"Now," crowed Paddy, "at least we'll leave the planet, for the surface will rotate away from under us."

"Zhri Khainga will see us leave," said Fay. "He'll know what we're doing and he'll find us as easily as if we were crawling on our hands and knees in the snow."

Paddy reached out, seized a stanchion, squeezed it. "If this were only his neck," he said between his teeth, "I'd hang on while his heels pounded on the deck and laugh in his face."

Fay laughed wanly. "This is no time for day-dreaming, Paddy dear." She looked out the port. "We've already risen about a foot from the ground."

Paddy narrowed his eyes thoughtfully. "I know how to get a kick out of those tubes. It'll cost us a million marks and it'll give us a nasty jar, since there's no counter-gravity to the acceleration—but we'll do it."

"Do what, Paddy?"

"We have four drive tubes on this little hull. There's lots of energy curled up and slumbering inside each one of them. Now if we let that energy come whirling out the after end we'll go forward. Of course, we'll ruin the tube."

"Do you know how, Paddy?" Fay asked doubtfully.

"I think I'll just shoot the end of the tube loose and it'll be like breaking open a fire hose." He looked out the port. "Now we're six feet off the ground—and look! there's that Koton! See him? Sitting there as calm and majestic as you please, laughing at us. Here give me that gun, I'll make a Christian of him—and I'll shoot off our tube at the same time."

He snapped the bubble back over his head, stepped into the lock, opened the outer port. Zhri Khainga quickly ducked behind a rock and Paddy regretfully held his fire. He turned, braced himself, drew a bead on the tip of the lower tube, gritted his teeth, commended himself to his natal saint and squeezed the trigger.

The tube split, an instantaneous spiral of blue flame lashed out, smote the ground. The boat lunged ahead, up at a slant.

Fay painfully got down from the elastic webbing, ran to the port. "*Paddy!*" She looked through the bull's-eye in the lock, heart in her mouth.

Paddy lay crumpled, unconscious. The bubble around his head was cracked; air was whistling out—

visibly, as the water vapor condensed to fog. Blood was trickling from his nose, spreading along his face.

"Paddy!" cried Fay as if her soul were dissolving. She could not close the outer door as his leg hung out, twisted at an odd angle. She could not open the inner door lest she lose all the air inside the ship.

She bent her forehead into the palms of her hands, whimpered. Then rising, she ran to the air-suit rack. One leg—both legs—zip up the side—head bubble, two snaps. She ran to the lock, tugged it open against the inner pressure and the blast of air nearly flung her out into space.

She caught hold of Paddy's arm, pulled his weightless body in against the dying current of air.

"Paddy," whispered Fay. "Are you dead?"

There was air in the cabin, warm clear air. Paddy lay on his bunk, one leg in a splint, a bandage around his head. Fay sat mopping at the trickle of blood which seeped from his nose.

Paddy sighed, shook in a delirium. Fay gave him a third injection of vivest-101, and spoke to him soothingly in a voice soft as summer grass.

Paddy gave a sudden jerk, then sighed, relaxed. Fay bent over him. "Paddy?" He breathed, he slept.

Fay arose, went to the port. Delta Trianguli was a small cold ball of light astern, the planet inconspicuous among brighter stars.

Three days passed. There had come no cruising shark of a Koton ship. Perhaps they were safe. Perhaps Zhri Khainga preferred the thought of his golden sheets to revenge.

Paddy awoke on the fourth day. "Fay," he muttered.

"Yes, Paddy dear."

"Where are we?"

"We're safe, Paddy, I hope."

"Still no power?"

"Not yet. But I found what happened and we can fix it as soon as you get well. I'm trying to pull it apart—a busbar that was shorted and fused. It made a terrible mess."

Paddy lay still a moment. His face twitched, his mouth pulled up at the corners in a grimace. He said, as if to himself, "Whatever happens, it's the Son that did it to himself and his own people. It was his own treachery, his own fault, and none of mine...."

Fay bent over him anxiously. "What do you mean, Paddy?"

Paddy muttered, "I planned all the time to tell him, since I'm no murderer, before he ever used the sheets."

"What did you do?"

Paddy sighed, turned his head away. "There's a wealth of destruction in a dot, Fay—a little dot."

Fay peered at his face. Was he asleep? No.

"Paddy, what are you talking about?"

"Fay," said Paddy weakly, "the space-drive has been my fascination ever since I first heard about it and it's like to been my death—twice, three, four, a dozen times. And one of the times was on Akhabats, where in my ignorance I thought I could burrow into the manifolding shop and curl them out by the dozen.

"I found that it wasn't so simple but a very delicate matter. Power floods into the tube from one end and there's fifteen coils and they pound it and kneed it and bind it and curl it like a big kick-hammer.

"When all the strengths are just right that great energy snarls and fights but it winds around on itself and there it stops—a tight little core of space-warp.

But if one of the coils is off, then there's a weak spot and all the energy breaks out and knocks the world apart.

"When I tried my hand at it on Akhabats there wasn't any power in the line except a bit of static charge but the kick nearly blasted away the shop."

"So?" asked Fay breathlessly.

"So—when Zhri Khainga, the Koton, pulls the switch—all hell will break loose."

"But Paddy," whispered Fay, "why? Those were the sheets we got from the dead Sons."

"There's two little decimal points that make the difference, Fay. Two little dots. On the Badau and the Loristan sheets, the duplicated numbers. I had just time for it. Two little marks."

She straightened from her bent position, looked away.

"It was to be our ace in the hole," said Paddy. "Sure I'd have told him about it over space-wave once we got clean away because I'm no hand for the killing, Fay. But now whatever happens is through himself since he cut off our power and it's his hard luck."

"It's the ninth day, Paddy," said Fay.

"Humph. Two days for the ship to pick him up, four days back to Montras, three days. It should be time for news."

He turned on the receiver, functioning feebly from the power of the cell in his flashlight.

A Shaul spoke, and they strained their ears to hear.

"Attention—word from Zhri Khainga, Son of Lang-try from Koto. Paddy Blackthorn, the convict and assassin, has been killed on a dead planet hideout by a Koton patrol ship. No further details have been released. Thus the greatest manhunt in the history of space comes to an end and interest traffic returns to normal."

"Is that all then?" Paddy asked pettishly. "Merely that I'm dead? Sure that would be no news to me were it true. I'd be the first to know it. Are there no explosions, no disasters? Is Zhri Khainga so cautious that he doesn't trust the data of his father and his unhealthy uncles? Why does he wait then?"

"Hush, Paddy dear," said Fay. "You'll excite yourself. Let's get back to our work. In another day we'll be repaired and send a warning message."

"Och," said Paddy. "The suspense is killing me. Why doesn't he drop the other shoe?"

Exclaimed Paddy, "The news. Fay, it's time for the news."

Fay wiped her face with a greasy hand. "If you'd wait ten minutes we'd be done. There's just the clip and welding to be done on that gang switch, and then we'd get the news on ship's power."

Paddy limped unheeding to the receiver and the thin whistle of space-wave sang through the cabin. Then, *gong, gong, gong!* rang the speaker—deep doleful sounds.

In a kind of numb attentiveness they heard the voice. "...stupendous crater...millions dead...for the dead Son, Zhri Khainga..."

Fay turned off the speaker. "Well, there it is. Don't worry any more. It's done. There goes Zhri Khainga and all his nerve-suits."

"I wouldn't have had it that way," said Paddy dully.

She stepped over to him, took his face in her two small hands. "Look here, Paddy Blackthorn, I'm tired of your moping! Now you come help me put in that switch. Then we'll fly home to Earth."

Paddy sighed, stood up, threw his arms around her. "That will be wonderful, Fay."

"First we'll get rid of this space-drive information and then—"

"And then we'll be married. We'll buy up all of County Cork," said Paddy with mounting enthusiasm. "We'll build a house a mile long and as high as necessary and champagne will flow out of every spigot. We'll raise the finest horses ever seen at Dublin Meet and the lords of the universe will tip their caps to us."

"We'll get fat, Paddy."

"Nonsense! And once a year we'll climb into our space-boat and we'll visit all our scenes of adventure again, just for old time's sake. Akhabats, Spade-Ace, the Langtry planets—and this time they'll be running after us, hoping for the privilege of carrying our bags."

"And don't forget the Angry Dragon, Paddy," said Fay. "We could visit there and be all alone. But now—"

"But now?"

A minute later Fay stood back breathless. "First, that switch! Now you get back to work, Paddy Blackthorn. There's only ten more minutes of it, and then we're home for Earth."